FEAR OF DROWNING

Peter Turnbull

St. Martin's Minotaur ✹ New York

FEAR OF DROWNING. Copyright © 1999 by Peter Turnbull.
All rights reserved. Printed in the United States of America.
No part of this book may be used or reproduced in any
manner whatsoever without written permission except in the
case of brief quotations embodied in critical articles or reviews.
For information, address St. Martin's Press, 175 Fifth Avenue,
New York, N.Y. 10010.

The word 'snickelways' is used with permission of Mark W. Jones

www.minotaurbooks.com

ISBN 0-312-26158-6

First published in Great Britain by Collins Crime,
HarperCollins*Publishers*

First St. Martin's Minotaur Edition: August 2000

10 9 8 7 6 5 4 3 2 1

1

Tuesday morning

  ... in which the alarum is sounded.

He was unsure exactly when it came about, exactly when
it occurred, but at some point, the very ordinariness of it
became suspicious.

For the third successive evening, the lights in the Williamses'
bungalow, the living room light and the bedroom light, went
on at the same time – at the same time each evening and also
at the same time as each other – and then two hours later
went off at the same time, at the same time each evening,
at the same time as each other. The man at first thought it
only careless to arrange the timing switches so that the lights
in the house go on and off at the same time. Far more sensible,
he thought, to stagger them, as was his practice, ensuring that
the light in the bedroom was off half an hour after the light in
the living room. For the first night that the house was clearly
unoccupied, all was normal. The Williamses were out for the
evening. Out with their son home from the navy and their
daughter up from London for the weekend. The two sports
cars in the drive and the absence of the Williamses' Volvo
estate said so. That had been the Saturday evening and the
man had noticed the lights of the bungalow go on as he
walked his dog past the building. Later that night he was
putting the empty milk bottles out on his front step when he
caught sight of the Williamses' bungalow through the small
copse which separated his house from their bungalow, just as

the lights in both rooms went out at the same time, almost, perhaps thirty seconds between the living room light going out and the bedroom light also going out. But to all intents and purposes, he thought, they went out at the same time and so telegraphed a clear signal to any potential burglar that the property was unoccupied. The man remained indoors all the following Sunday, leaving his home only in the evening to exercise his dog, walking him the mile and a half to the Horse and Hounds in the next village, a pint of beer before last orders and the mile and a half back. Three miles a day, good for man, good for dog. He glanced at the Williamses' bungalow as he walked past and saw that the two sports cars had gone and the Williamses' Volvo parked in the drive, though not as it usually was parked. Usually, it was reversed in and left nearer the road than the house. When he saw it on the Sunday, it had been fronted in and left close to the garage doors. As he passed the bungalow again at approximately 11.15 p.m. on the return leg of his evening walk, he noticed the lights go out, one after the other, as an owl hooted from a nearby wood; the only sound on the rich summer's evening.

The man did not look for the Williamses on the Monday, but whenever he was in a place in his house, or in his garden, that allowed him to see the Williamses' bungalow, he would stop and observe it for a few seconds, hoping to catch a glimpse of the ebullient Max or of the soft-spoken Amanda, as he had come to know them in the short time that they had been neighbours. But there was still nothing to be alarmed about, he didn't know them well enough to know their habits, their daily routine, and it was summer, the time when people take their holidays. But he did know that Max, who had described himself as a 'financier' when he had come to introduce himself, worked at home, and so far as he could tell, Amanda was not employed. And, also so far as he could tell, they used their car each day, lazily so, for he had seen Amanda drive away and return ten minutes later and enter their home clutching a loaf of bread. Nothing yet to be alarmed about, but a worry nagged in his mind. So much so that when that evening he walked his dog to the Horse and Hounds he stopped outside the Williamses' house and looked at the building for about ten minutes, hoping to catch a glimpse of one or the other, or both. But he saw nothing and on his return journey, he, being a man of habit, passed the bungalow just as the lights in the living room and the bedroom went out at the same time. More or less.

It was the Tuesday morning, at about ten o'clock, that the man acted out of concern because, by then, what had been normal had become suspicious. He walked slowly up the drive, and pressed the doorbell by the front porch door, noting uncollected post lying inside the porch. The bell rang the Westminster chimes and echoed loudly in the bungalow but produced no reaction.

'Not right,' he said to himself as much as to his Labrador. 'Not right at all.'

He returned to his house and phoned the police and asked that they attend the bungalow, the last house on Old Pond Road in the village of Bramley on Ouse. He explained why and said he'd make himself known to the constable. He returned to the grass verge outside the Williamses' house and enjoyed a pipe while he waited for the police to arrive. He had finished a large bowl of St Bruno, enjoying the flat, lush landscape, dotted here and there with small woods, but in the main, fields of green or yellow, and a few, he thought too few, hedgerows, when the area car arrived.

''Morning,' he said cheerfully to the constable.

''Morning, sir.'

'It was myself who phoned you.' The man had long stopped wondering at the youth of police officers.

'Yes, sir. Worried about a household, I believe?'

'This one here.'

'Oh, yes?' For his part, the officer saw a genial-looking man in his late middle years, relaxed in light-coloured trousers, a T-shirt and a wide-brimmed cricket hat. He also noted the black Labrador sitting patiently at his side and detected a strong bond between man and dog. 'What appears to be the problem?'

'Well, I hope nothing, but I haven't seen my neighbours

since Saturday. I don't know them very well, they moved in only about . . . well, I'll tell you . . . June now, they arrived after Easter, so . . .'

'Just a few weeks then?'

'Yes. Not sufficient for me to get to know them, so I don't know their routine, except that he works from home and they tend to go everywhere by car. So not being seen for a day or two and the car not having moved, and also parked unusually.'

'Unusually?'

'They normally reverse it into the drive and leave it closer to the road than the house.'

'Do you know their names, sir?'

'Williams. Max and Amanda, couple in their fifties, late fifties.'

'And you last saw them on Saturday?'

'About three o'clock. Their adult children visited. The son is an officer in the Royal Navy, their daughter is a civil servant and normally lives in London. They did tell me once that when their son and daughter visit they invariably go to the Mill.'

'The Mill?'

'It's a restaurant, well out of *my* price range, but they enthused about it. It's near Stamford Bridge. I noticed two sports cars in the drive on Saturday evening, they'd gone by the Sunday evening and the Volvo was parked in the drive, but not, as I said, as it usually is. I assume that their children had visited and they had gone for a meal, as is their wont on such occasions. I caught a glimpse of Amanda on the Saturday afternoon, just caught a glimpse of her as she entered the house, but nothing since. I don't want to be alarmist, they could be on holiday . . . the lights are going on and off as if on timer switches, there is uncollected post . . . they have a glass-panelled porch, as you see.'

'I think you're right to be concerned, sir. Sorry, your name is . . . ?'

'Thom. T.H.O.M. Schoolmaster, retired. History.'

4

The constable wrote on his pad. 'And your address, Mr Thom?'

'Number twenty-six, Old Pond Road. That's my house there.' He turned and pointed to his house. 'Next property to the Williamses', they're twenty-eight, Old Pond Road, the last house in the village on this road, not a building beyond their bungalow on this road until you get to Upper Leemans, a mile and a half distant. Me and my best friend here do that walk each day. We do it in the evening this time of year. He's a black dog, as you see, and, like all black dogs, he suffers dreadfully in the heat. That's when I thought something was odd, walking past the Williamses' on our way home, the lights went out at about eleven-fifteen on successive evenings.'

'Any other neighbours share your concern?'

'I am the only neighbour really. The people across the street are away and have been for a week or so. You see, they have asked me to keep an eye on their property, which I am pleased to do. I don't know the Williamses well, but we are on friendly enough terms for them to be able to ask me to keep an eye on their house if they went away for a few days. Which all adds to my worry. The thing to do, I would suggest with utmost respect, is to contact their son.'

'He's in the navy?'

'Yes, by sheer coincidence, he's shore-based at Knaresborough. At least, he was when Max and Amanda moved in. Could have been posted on by now, of course, but he's not so distant that he can't come home for the weekend. Max told me about their son when they moved in. Anyway, it's over to you, but I feel better for having reported it.'

'You were right to do so. I'll go and have a closer look at the building. If there's nothing out of the ordinary, I think I will take up your suggestion and phone the Andrew.'

'The Andrew?'

'The navy.'

'George.'

'Sir?' Hennessey looked up at the small, for a police officer,

5

dapper, immaculately groomed man who stood in the door frame of his office.

'Got a disappearance, I hear?'

'Yes, sir.'

'Anything in it, you think?' Commander Sharkey held an old-looking book in his hands.

'Too early in the piece to say yet, sir.' Hennessey picked up the phone. 'Just contacting the relatives now.'

'I see.' Sharkey approached Hennessey's desk. 'Actually, I just stopped by to show you this. I found it in a charity shop, it's a first-hand account of the Battle of Waterloo.'

'Oh . . .' Hennessey took the book from Sharkey. 'How interesting.'

'Knowing your interest, I thought that would be right up your street.'

'I'll read it this evening, sir. Thank you. I'll let you have it back as soon as.'

'Oh no, keep it. It hardly cost me anything, a few pence . . . I can run to that.' Sharkey paused. 'Speaking of pence . . . you'll let me know if . . .'

'Sir.' George Hennessey smiled. 'Please don't worry . . . about the corruption, I mean. If there is anything going on, I'll know and I'll be the first to tell you.'

'Yes.' Sharkey nodded. 'It's just that I saw enough of that in Hong Kong to last a lifetime, enough to see me well out.'

'Sir, believe me. There's nothing, nothing for you to worry about. This isn't Hong Kong. We are not in anybody's pocket.'

'Thanks, George. That's a great comfort. I mean that.' Sharkey left the room looking, thought Hennessey, a relieved man. He continued to dial the number. 'Good morning, sir,' he said when his call was answered.

'Morning, Lieutenant Home-Dawson, Officer Watch One.'

'Chief Inspector Hennessey, North Yorkshire Police.'

'Yes, sir.'

'Wonder if you could help us?'

'If we can.' The speaker was a young-sounding, confident-sounding man.

'Do you have a Lieutenant Williams with you at present?'

6

'We might.'

'I see. I can understand your caution. I might be anybody.'

'Quite,' but said with good humour.

'Well, should you have a Lieutenant Williams stationed with you at the moment, would you be good enough to ask him to phone myself, please, Chief Inspector Hennessey, Micklegate Bar Police Station in York?' Hennessey relayed the phone number. He added, 'You could tell him not to be worried, it may well be nothing to be concerned about.'

'Very good, sir. He'll appreciate that.'

Hennessey replaced the phone and glanced out of his office window at Micklegate Bar, where the severed heads of traitors, rebels and enemies of the Crown were once displayed. He glanced at his office, the police mutual calendar and the Home Office issue filing cabinet, of battleship grey. It was, he felt, a dull, hard, cold office but any softening would be frowned on by the police authority. He had on occasion visited other places of work, offices in the private sector and the public sector, and had been envious of the comfort offered by a potted plant or a poster of a faraway place. He stood and made himself a mug of coffee in the detective constables' room, carried the steaming mug of liquid through to his office and sat sipping it as he leafed through memos, reading each one and then initialling it to denote that he had 'read and absorbed it' and then returned them to the wire basket prior to carrying the basket of memos through to the detective constables' room for each officer there to read and initial the memos. Then his phone rang.

'Hennessey,' he said as he snatched it up.

'Phone call for you, sir,' said a nervous young woman on the switchboard. 'A Lieutenant Williams.'

'Oh yes. Put him through please . . . hello . . . Lieutenant Williams?'

'Speaking.' The voice was cold and aloof. Quite, quite different, thought Hennessey, from the warmth and friendliness of Lieutenant Home-Dawson. He also thought that Williams

7

sounded older. Somehow, the enthusiasm of Home-Dawson did not extend to Williams.

'Thank you for coming back to me so soon.' Hennessey leaned forward in his chair and rested his elbows on the desk top.

'Shore-based,' Williams said, and Hennessey picked up a sour note in his voice. He found it interesting, always having believed that a good measure of a person can be taken from their speaking voice, and because of this valued 'meeting' people by means of telephone. Here was sourness. 'Sailing a desk,' Williams continued. 'You tend to be a little more accessible than you would be if you were at sea.'

'Where a sailor belongs?'

'I'll say. But you wanted me to phone you?'

'Yes. It's concerning your parents.'

'My parents?'

'They are Max and Amanda Williams of Old Pond Road in –?'

'Yes. Yes. Those are they.'

'We responded to a call from a concerned neighbour, this morning, who reported that he has not seen your parents since Saturday last, but would in the course of events expect to see them near daily, by all accounts. I didn't attend myself.'

'They should be at home.'

'Well, this is the reason for my call. I didn't want to force entry if they were on holiday, for example.'

'Yes . . . but no . . . they should be there.' A note of concern crept into Williams's voice. 'Could I ask you to go and have a look inside the house?'

'Is there a key?'

'In the garage. The garage door is held on a latch but isn't locked as such. Shelf right-hand side, two glass jars full of paraffin and nuts and bolts. Between the two jars . . . it's just above head height, can't see the key but you can reach it very easily. It's the key to the back door of the bungalow. If you come to need the front door key that'll be hanging up in the kitchen.'

8

'We'll get back to you.' Hennessey replaced the phone and shouted, 'Sergeant Yellich!'

'Yes, boss?'

Hennessey stood and reached for his hat as Yellich came into his office.

'I want you to take a couple of constables and make a brief search at this address; twenty-eight, Old Pond Road, Bramley on Ouse. It's a village, north of York off the A19.'

'Yes, boss.' Yellich nodded vigorously.

'Two middle-aged householders reported missing. Their son says they should be at home. There's a key for the back door in the garage.' Hennessey told him exactly where. 'Go and see what you find, but tread carefully. Even if you don't find anything immediately suspicious, still treat it as a crime scene.'

''Course, boss. You're not coming?'

'No. I'm going to have some lunch.'

Sergeant Yellich, followed by two constables, entered the Williamses' bungalow by the rear door, having located the key exactly where they had been told it would be found. Inside, 28, Old Pond Road revealed itself to be a bungalow of even more modest proportions than was suggested by the modest exterior lines. The kitchen Yellich found to be small and cramped, the main bedroom had space only for the double bed and a dressing table and wardrobe. The living room and dining room seemed swamped by the furniture they contained, so much so that Yellich was put in mind of the new build estates, the show houses of which have scaled-down furniture: buy one and then try making the double bed fit into the bedroom. The bungalow was kept neatly, to an everything-in-its-place perfection. The only thing possibly out of place was the *Sunday Times* 'Culture' section, left sprawling on the settee opened at last Saturday's television listings. A small alcove off the dining room had been turned into a study, with a bureau pushed in sideways and a chair hard up against it for want of floor space, so that any person sitting on the chair would have to have his, or her, legs splayed on either side of it. Yellich lifted up the bureau lid and found the interior to be a neat ordering of documents and papers. Nothing appeared to have been touched. There was no sign of violence, no sign of unlawful entry. And most importantly, there were no dead bodies. A neat, well-ordered house; clean too, thought Yellich. Very clean, a strong smell of bleach and disinfectant, perhaps accentuated by the hothouse effect of all windows and doors being shut on a succession of very hot days. That would cause a staleness of the air and enhance odours. The garden too, like the house, was kept to millimetre-exact perfection: a neat lawn, a weedless border in which grew flowers. A garden hut stood to one side of the lawn. He returned his attention to the interior of the house. He found a cheque book in the joint names of Max and Amanda Williams. On the dressing table in the bedroom, he found a ladies' watch and a little hard cash, about twenty pounds, he guessed. He also found a ladies' handbag, cluttered with possessions. Clearly the handbag in present use by the lady of the house. This worried him. It was his observation that women do not go far without their handbag. Not voluntarily anyway.

The house, he decided, was a crime scene. He left one constable and a car at the house, in the front drive, and returned to Micklegate Bar with the other constable. He opened a 'mis per' file on Max and Amanda Williams. He then phoned HMS Halley, Knaresborough, and asked to speak to Lieutenant Williams. He told the lieutenant what he had found and obtained a description of Max and Amanda Williams.

Having lunched to his great satisfaction at the fish restaurant on Lendal, Hennessey walked the walls back to Micklegate Bar, joining the ancient battlements at Lendal Bridge. The walls were crowded with tourists who weaved skilfully in and out of each other, and again he thought, as he often did on such occasions, that the York Tourist Board would be well advised to introduce a one-way system for the walking of the walls, at least in the summer months. He fell in behind a party of schoolchildren, about thirty in number, about twelve years of age, all sensibly, he thought, dressed in yellow T-shirts and scarlet baseball-style caps, making each very conspicuous for the four teachers he saw to be in charge of the group. Very, very sensible in such a crowded city. To his right across Station Road was the railway station with its expensive canopy, which when it was built in 1877, was the largest structure in the world. To his left he could discern the roof and platform of the original station which was built 'within the walls'. The original archways for which he could identify under Queen Street as it climbed up to Micklegate Bar. Hennessey enjoyed working in York, though it was not his native city. He enjoyed its compactness, especially of the city centre, really the size of a small town, but benefiting from being steeped in history, an important town from Roman times to the present day, with a magnificent minster, one of the great churches of Europe, which was allowed to dominate the townscape. No angular high-rises here. The prestigious university, he thought, diplomatically placed on the edge of the town, in parkland with lakes and wide spaces and of brick buildings of only medium-rise proportions. Sometimes the underside of York, less pleasant, would reveal itself, when the agricultural workers or the miners came into town on a Saturday evening, wanting their beer. But Hennessey was well content to work in the city and live a little way outside it. He left the walls at Micklegate Bar and entered the narrow entrance of the police station. He checked his pigeonhole, just a handwritten note from Sergeant Yellich, who felt the bungalow at 28, Old Pond Road, Bramley on Ouse, ought to merit the status of crime scene, and he had opened a missing persons file in the first instance in respect of Max and Amanda Williams. He went to the CID rooms and found Yellich in his office, sitting with his feet up on his desk, eating sandwiches and reading an early edition of the *Yorkshire Evening Post*.

'Sandwiches again, Yellich?'

'My wife makes them up, boss. Cheap and convenient.'

'Haven't you noticed that they make you sleepy in the afternoon? All those enzymes.'

'What, boss?'

'Enzymes, Yellich, enzymes. It's the stuff in bread that makes you sleepy. My office when you're ready.' Hennessey returned to his office. He had avoided eating bread at lunchtime since that terrible day very early in his career when, as a young constable, he had eaten sandwiches in the police canteen and had a few hours later fallen asleep in the rear of an airless court, his snores bringing on an acid comment from His Honour, followed the next morning by an 'interview' with the Chief Constable. But he had observed that the best lessons in life are often the hardest learned, and had from that day hence avoided bread at lunchtime and found himself exhorting others to do the same. He lowered himself into his chair as Yellich appeared at the doorway of his office, mug of tea in one hand, the last of a sandwich in the other.

'Take a pew, Yellich. The Williamses' house.'

'Yes, boss.'

'Just finish your sandwich and let me have your impressions of it.'

'Neat,' said Yellich, with food in his mouth. He swallowed. 'Very neat. Wouldn't like to live there.'

'Not a place where a man could put his feet up, speak with his mouth full and feel at home?'

Yellich didn't reply.

'But no sign of violence?'

'No, boss.'

'Forced entry?'

'No. Nothing at all like that.'

'And no bodies?'

'No, boss.'

'Yet you think it's a crime scene?'

'Aye, I do, boss.' Yellich leaned back in his chair. He was a man in his thirties, short, dark hair, balanced features, clean-shaven.

'Why?'

'Well, boss, the son says they should be there, there was cash and a cheque book in the house, things which would

12

not be left if they were going away for any length of time, the cheque book especially. The neighbour; Mr Thom, he told the constable that they don't go anywhere without their car, they'd only leave their car, I suppose, if they were going on a foreign holiday, or suchlike.'

'And we'd know if they were on a planned period of absence. Go on, you're convincing me.'

'It's out of character. By all accounts. A well-set-up couple in middle age, wealthy enough to run a Volvo estate and live in a smart bungalow – bit cramped inside, but smart enough – don't vanish into thin air.'

'Do we know them?'

'No. I ran their names and approximate ages through the computer as a matter of course. Negative.'

'So, no criminal acquaintances that we know of.'

'No, boss.'

'And they're known to dine at the Mill, according to their neighbour. So they've got money and successful children. I have to say that you're right, Sergeant, I too feel that all is not well, not well at all. My waters tell me.'

'Aye, sir?'

'Aye, Yellich, aye. You and I have two places to visit.'

'We have, boss?'

'We have. First you wash your sandwich down with another of the obligatory mugs of tea, and make me one while you're at it.'

'So, where are we going?' Yellich stood.

'We're going to a stone frigate.'

'A what?'

'That's what the navy call their shore establishments, and then we're going to the Mill.'

HMS Halley stood off the A6055 Knaresborough to Borough-bridge Road, it was surrounded by a wire fence and shrubs and signs warning of dog patrols. Hennessey drove his car up to the main gate and halted. A young sailor, carrying a machine pistol, approached the driver's side of Hennessey's car. 'Good afternoon, gentlemen.' His manner was polite but serious.

''Morning, son.' Hennessey thought the man too young to be carrying a gun. 'North Yorkshire Police to see Lieutenant Williams.'

'Yes, sir. Do you have ID?'

The officers showed their identity cards.

'If you'd like to wait here, please, gentlemen.' The young sailor returned to the gatehouse and was seen by Hennessey and Yellich to pick up a phone, speak briefly and then listen for a longer period than the time he spent talking, and then replace the phone. He didn't leave the gatehouse nor even glance at Hennessey and Yellich, who sat in the car listening to the sounds of the summer foliage, the birdsong, the occasional rustling as a small animal moved over dried vegetation. Beyond the gatepost the drive led to rows of huts and a parade ground on which a white ensign hung limply on a mast. Above was an expanse of blue, with few clouds, and a jet plane's vapour trail, high, very high up, and disappearing rapidly.

Eventually a dark-blue Land Rover approached the gate from within the base, shimmering through a heat haze. As it drew closer the police officers were able to make out the words 'Provost Marshal' painted on a sign which was bolted to the Land Rover's front bumper. The vehicle halted at the main gate and the occupant of the passenger seat got out of the vehicle and approached Hennessey and Yellich, while the driver executed a rapid three-point turn.

'I understand you gentlemen wish to see Mr Williams?' The member of the provost marshal's corps leaned forwards as he spoke to Hennessey.

'We do.'

'Have to ask you to leave your vehicle here, sir, we're on Bikini Amber because of terrorist activity in London.'

'I see.'

'Apart from anything else, it means that no civilian vehicles are allowed on Ministry land.'

'Fair enough.' Hennessey got out of the car. Yellich did likewise. They followed the man to the Land Rover and climbed, as invited, into the rear of the vehicle. Hennessey felt strange that his car should be seen as civilian. He felt it odd to be a civilian, to be seen as a civilian, after all, did not the police now refer to folk as civilians rather than members of the public, as was the case in his early years? He did not think it boded well for his retirement, which loomed, he felt, like a shortening shadow.

The Land Rover started with a jolt and sped across the base, halting, precisely, it seemed to Hennessey and Yellich, not an inch out of place. They alighted outside the provost marshal's office, by the sign by the door. A raised wooden platform stood by the door on which a young rating stood, rigidly in the 'at ease' position. Hennessey and Yellich couldn't help but look at the man, a boy really, and both noted how pale and fearful he seemed.

Hennessey and Yellich were shown into a room in which stood a steel table and three chairs, two on one side of the table, the third facing them on the other side. There was no other furniture or fittings in the room. The light bulb was naked, the floor was of brown tile, heavily disinfected, the walls and the ceiling were whitewashed.

'Some interview room,' Yellich growled. 'It makes me feel guilty just being here.'

Hennessey didn't reply, but thought that Yellich had a point; the room, he felt, would make a saint confess to something. Not for the Ministry of Defence the niceties of the Police and Criminal Evidence Act, the recorded interviews and the presence of a solicitor.

Outside the building a strong-sounding, assertive football was heard approaching. The boy on the platform was heard to snap to attention, a door opened and three pairs of boots similarly snapped to attention. A clipped voice said, 'Good afternoon, sir. Interview room one, sir.' Hennessey and Yellich had just time to glance at each other before Lieutenant Rufus Williams R.N. entered the room. He revealed himself to be a powerfully built man in his thirties with glaring eyes.

'Lieutenant Williams?' Hennessey asked.

'Yes. And you are?'

15

'Chief Inspector Hennessey. This is Sergeant Yellich. We spoke on the phone this morning.'

'Yes.'

'Shall we sit down?' Hennessey spoke softly, he wanted to resist being drawn into Williams's snappy naval way of speaking. He found it oddly contagious, as if waking a ghost in him. He also wanted to control the interview. A look of anger flashed across Williams's eyes, as if angry that Hennessey should take the initiative about whether to sit or not. But he said, 'Yes, if you like.'

Hennessey and Yellich sat side by side facing Williams. Hennessey took out his notebook and allowed his eyes to wander. Yellich kept his eyes fixed on Williams.

'Well, Lieutenant, I'm afraid we have some bad news for you.'

'Oh?'

'Your parents appear to have disappeared.'

'Disappeared?'

'I'm afraid so. The circumstances are sufficiently mysterious for us to be concerned and we're being more proactive than we would be in a normal mis per enquiry because of it.'

'I'm pleased to hear it.'

'We entered your parents' bungalow – we found the key where you said it would be. There is no sign of violence in the house, no damage that we can see, no sign of anything having been stolen . . . there was a little cash on the dressing table . . . if there had been a theft of any kind that is likely to have been stolen.'

'Fair enough.' Williams's eyes had a steely glint. Little wonder, Hennessey thought, that the boy on the platform looked so nervous. 'I suppose that would have been swept up and pocketed by a thief.'

'Everything was neat and tidy. The only thing a little out of place is the fact that your parents' car is parked in what is an unusual way. So we're told. Apparently, both Mr and Mrs Williams were in the habit of reversing the car into the driveway, but it has been parked having been fronted in. But it's dangerous to read anything into that. When did you last see your parents?'

'Both of them on Saturday night/Sunday morning. We got home from the restaurant at about half past midnight, went straight to our beds. I last saw Mother on the Sunday morning, Father was sleeping off his hangover. We had been out for a meal that night, me, my sister, Mother and Father. On the Sunday we all slept late, as we usually do when we've been out.'

'Do you often go out as a family?'

'Not often, once every three months, possibly more than that. That was the first time we had been out as a family since my parents moved to the bungalow, in March, I think it was . . . and the last time we went out for a meal was in February, for Mother's birthday.'

'I see. Was the meal on Saturday evening to mark a special occasion?'

'No.'

'So you left on the Sunday, you saw your mother but not your father?'

'That's correct.'

'What about your sister? Did she see your father on the Sunday?'

'You'll have to ask her that. I left before she did. I have much less distance to travel but I wanted to return home.'

'Convenient that you're based so close to your parents?'

'Well, it helps or it hinders, depends on your attitude to service life. Some have made the grade in the services because they've been posted a long way from their roots, others have survived because they've been able to return home at frequent intervals. It's a question of personality.'

'And you?'

'I like it. I wasn't always shore-based. I was at sea for a few years, then I was shore-based. It suits me being close to York.'

'What sort of establishment is this?'

'Can't tell you, but as things go it's not so important. We won't win or lose the next war because of HMS Halley.'

17

'You're not happy at this base?'

'I'm happy with the location.'

'But not the position itself?'

'No. I've had happier times.'

'I see. Can I ask how old you are?'

'Thirty-five. What's the relevance of that?'

'I don't know if it is relevant or not. But your parents have disappeared, I'm afraid we must begin to assume the worst. Your parents are how old?'

'Both fifty-eight years.'

'Young parents, then?'

'Yes . . . I suppose they were.'

'I see.'

'Do you ever say anything else but "I see".'

'Only when I don't see, sir. Then I say I don't. You see? So your relationship with your parents was good?'

'Yes . . . no more issues than any other family.'

'It sounds like it . . . regular, if infrequent meals out, sounds like a successful family. And your sister, she too has a good relationship with your parents?'

'Well, yes . . . closer to Mother than Father. She's a year younger than me.' Williams seemed to Hennessey to be relaxing.

'Not married?'

'No. It worries my parents, they want her to find someone and start a family. Me too, but being a man nature allows us more time . . . but they're worried about Nicky. Thirty-four and still single . . . good-looking girl too . . . no reason for her not to marry . . . clever girl . . . went to university . . . works in the Civil Service in London.'

'I see. Do you know her address off hand?'

'Twelve D, Chertsey Mews, NW2.'

Hennessey scribbled on his notepad. 'Nice and central.'

'Yes. You know London?'

'I ought to. I am a Londoner.'

'I noticed you didn't have a Yorkshire accent.'

'I grew up in Greenwich. You'll know Greenwich, being a naval officer?'

18

Williams smiled. 'Yes, Greenwich, the Naval College, the Observatory, the Maritime Museum . . . the Sailors' Hospital. Pleasant pubs as well.'

'Yes. I'm from down the bottom end of Trafalgar Road, near the hospital. Maze Hill, really.'

'I never got down there.'

'Navy never did, officers especially. But back to the matter in hand. Did your parents have any worries or concerns that you were aware of?'

'Not that I am aware of.'

'Did your father have enemies?'

'He is a businessman. All businessmen have enemies.'

'Any that stand out?'

'Not that I knew of. I didn't take much interest in Father's affairs.'

'What sort of business did he run?'

'No one sort. He had fingers in a lot of pies. He makes his money by investing in new companies, or buying newly floated shares. Venture capitalism, I believe it's called.'

'I see. And your parents' relationship itself, is that healthy?'

'Well, yes, very. They were happy together.'

'Can I ask a personal question?'

'I daresay.'

'You sister lives in NW2?'

'Yes.'

'Rent or mortgage?'

'Rent.'

'NW2 on a civil servant's salary?'

'Father was a generous man. He subsidized Nicola and myself. I can live off the base and enjoy a full social life because of Father. The salary I receive is a token payment. Service officers have to have private means.'

'Really?'

'Yes, really.'

'And you have suddenly begun speaking of your father in the past tense.'

'No, I haven't. His money is in the past tense. I suppose I should say that he *was* a businessman.'

'What do you mean?'

'He's broke.' Williams smiled. 'You think it's funny that I laugh? What else can I do? It's better than crying.'

'Lieutenant Williams, what do you think has happened to your parents?'

'I think they've done a moonlight flit.'

'When did you learn this?'

'Well, I've suspected for a while, but all our, that is mine and Nicky's, fears were confirmed on Saturday. That's why I didn't remain long at the house on Sunday morning. I wanted to get home. I was in a state of . . .'

'Anger?'

'No . . . numbness. Shock. My world closed in very suddenly on Saturday night.'

'I see.'

'I thought you'd say that.'

'When men go broke they often leave unpaid debts.'

'Yes. But I don't know if my father owed money.'

'What does it mean for you?'

'It means I shall have to leave the navy.'

'Bother you?'

'Yes. Not too bothered about leaving the Halley.' Williams looked disdainfully around him. 'But the navy . . . it's been my life since I was seventeen. Can't survive without father's money . . . so I'll have to resign and make my way in civilian life. Daresay I can do that if I have to, and it looks like I'll have to.'

2

Tuesday afternoon and evening

... in which Chief Inspector Hennessey enjoys a history lesson and expresses grave concerns.

'The Fulling mill appeared in England in the thirteenth century and this particular example is believed to date from the mid-fourteenth century. A Fulling mill consisted of an axel or spindle onto which were attached a row of spinning wheels. The axel was driven by water power. The original mill was covered by a shed in which the millers worked on a daily basis, returning home each evening. It was thus the first form of factory. As can be seen, the stream has now dried up but the banks and the bed of the stream are still discernible.'

Hennessey read the notice attached to the wall and then looked down through the glass plate which was mounted on a brick-built square and elevated above floor level to waist height. He saw a pale, grey, decayed length of timber about six feet in length which lay across a shallow trench. It was to his eyes, nothing he thought special to look at, the sort of thing he would glance at once and forget, but equally, the sort of thing which would send a medievalist into a paroxysm of ecstasy. He turned his attention to the wall and pondered the reproductions of eighteenth-century prints of fox-hunting scenes, the originals clearly having been painted in the days when it was believed horses leapt rather than ran when they galloped. Beside the fox-hunting scenes was a reproduction of a seventeenth-century map of Yorkshire with 'the most famous and faire Citie of Yorke defcribed', and Hennessey studied the map, tracing the towns along the route of the present A1. He envied Yellich the ability to sit so patiently still. Hennessey had always had a restless nature, really since adolescence, utterly unable to sit still.

The room itself was the entrance hallway of the Mill restaurant, tastefully decorated in maroon. The reception desk stood against the wall beside the Fulling mill display case. It had a low ceiling with the beams exposed. Hennessey thought the beams seemed original to the later building. Opposite the reception desk the wall was given over to a vast window which looked out onto a garden, then a green meadow on which a herd of Herefords grazed contentedly, then there was the river Derwent, and beyond that more pasture with the occasional clump of trees, and ultimately, a flat skyline and then the vast blue sky.

'Gentlemen.' The proprietor of the Mill beamed and bumbled into the reception area, hands outstretched, swarthy, sallow, olive-skinned, dark-haired, white teeth. 'How do you do? How can I help you?'

'I'm well, thank you.' Hennessey accepted the man's hand, as Yellich stood and also shook the man's hand. 'We'd like to ask you some questions, if we may?'

'Certainly, certainly.' The man's warmth did not seem, to Hennessey, to be diminishing. He thought him a man with a clear conscience. 'We can go to the dining room. It's empty at the moment.'

The dining room was a long, narrow room with a ceiling noticeably higher than that of the reception area. It had tables along the walls, but no room for tables in the centre of the floor.

'Rivers change course, you see,' said the man, indicating a table near the door. 'When we opened the restaurant, we commissioned a local historian to research the history of the building. It was she who discovered the original Fulling mill and wrote the notice for us. She also notified the academic historians at the university and they came and photographed the length of wood and took measurements of it. I confess I would have chopped it up for firewood, but they were all very excited about it. She found out that a larger watermill had been built over the site of the original Fulling mill when the river ran nearer the building than it does today. The watermill closed down in the nineteenth century, very early nineteenth century, couldn't compete with steam, and in the near two hundred years since it has closed, the river has migrated to its present course. Rivers do that, apparently. We bought the building as a ruin about five years ago and decided to build up the best restaurant in the Vale of York.'

'And have you?' Hennessey found himself liking the man.

'We think so.'

'We?'

'Me and my brother. I am Mario Vialli and my brother is Bruno Vialli. We are of Siena. My brother has studied under the most famous chefs in the world, and I am the business man. He has the kitchen and I have the office. Together, we do our very best for the customers. My brother has great flair but he is not a businessman. I, on the other hand, have inherited our dear mother's shrewdness.'

'Siena, you say?'

'Yes.'

'I have been there. I was there during the Palio.'

'Ah.'

'I didn't see anything, couldn't get near . . . the crowd was immense. As I recall, it was the horse of the *contrada* of the tortoise which won.'

'Ha! That is the enemy of our *contrada*. We are of the *contrada* of the horse. The best.'

'Of course.'

'So, how can I help the police?'

'On Saturday' – Hennessey allowed a serious tone to enter his voice – 'a family by the name of Williams were dining here. Parents and an adult son and daughter.'

'Yes.' Mario Vialli nodded. 'They sat at that table there. I know the Williamses well. Is there some problem?'

'Mr and Mrs Williams have disappeared, but there's worrying circumstances which makes us inclined to treat it with more gravity than we normally would treat a mis per, as we call it.'

'Oh . . .' Vialli appeared genuinely saddened, and seemed to Hennessey to be very much in the manner of Italians as Hennessey had found them, wearing their emotion on their sleeve. 'That is bad, bad . . . bad.'

'It's very worrying. You seem to know the Williamses well?'

'I do . . . Mr . . . ?'

'Hennessey. I'm sorry, I'm Chief Inspector Hennessey and this is Sergeant Yellich . . . we seem to have leapt straight into the conversation.'

'My fault, forgive me.'

'No, the fault is mine. But the Williamses . . .'

'They've been valued customers for about ten years. We had another restaurant before we opened the Mill and we brought many loyal customers with us when we opened.'

'The other restaurant was in this locality?'

'Yes. Not far from here.'

'Interesting. I had the impression that the Williamses were incomers to the Vale.'

'Oh, no. They did move address a month or two ago. I know that they moved recently because their names are on our gourmet list. Every two months we have a gourmet evening with a great chef. They have been to one or two gourmet evenings, but they did notify us of their change of address.'

'I see. What are they like as a family?'

'Very English. It amuses me to look at them, but I didn't mean that in a rude way. Occasionally you meet someone who is just his nationality . . . in Italian we would say "*quintessenza*".'

'Quintessential.'

'There is such a word in English? Quintessential? So?'

'Yes.'

'Well, that is the Williamses. Very warm, probably not as reserved as some English, but their walk . . . they way they sit, the way they use their cutlery. So English. A delight to

24

serve. The staff love them, for their manner as well as the generosity of their tips.'

'So, as a family?'

'Well, close, I think. Over the years I have observed them value each other's company. The son seemed angry about something but it didn't affect the other three, they seemed to be quite happy.'

'Angry?'

'Too strong a word. Something had been said to upset him. He left ahead of the others, only by a minute or two, but ahead . . . a little irritated perhaps. But Mr and Mrs Williams seemed happy and their daughter didn't seem upset. And they all drove home together in their car, left at about midnight. So their son wasn't so upset that he didn't ride home with them.'

'Not a family at war then?'

'Oh no.' Vialli paused.

'You have something to tell me, Mr Vialli?'

'How do you know?'

'I have been a policeman for a very long time. It's the best explanation I can offer.'

'Mrs Williams has been coming to the restaurant with a man who is not her husband.' Vialli spoke matter-of-factly. 'Not weekly or even monthly, but always on a Wednesday.'

'How long has this been going on?'

'Perhaps a year . . . longer. They have a "thing" between them.'

'Do you know who he is?'

'A man called Sheringham. He phones and books the table in his name.'

Yellich took out his notepad and wrote the name down.

'Can you describe him?'

'He's in his twenties. Much younger than she. Very muscular.'

As they walked from the restaurant across the gravel car park to where Hennessey had parked his car, Hennessey said, 'This is murder, Yellich. No, it's not. It's double murder.'

'Yes, boss.'

25

'You don't think so?'

'Too early to say. What now, boss, back to the station, write this up and then call it a day?'

'No. There's work to do.'

'It's past five o'clock, boss.'

Hennessey paused and held eye contact. 'There's work to do.'

'I've got a family to go home to, boss.'

'And I haven't, is that what you're saying? I've got nothing to go home to and so I'm working late to fill up an empty life and I'm selfish keeping you with me. Is that what you're saying?'

'I didn't mean that, boss.'

'Look, this is a murder enquiry. We haven't got our corpses yet, but we will. And it's a recent murder, at this stage every minute is precious. If we were investigating a murder of years ago then perhaps time wouldn't be so precious. But as it is, it's very precious. We're going back to the Williamses' house. I'll take the most direct route and we'll time it.'

'Thirty-five minutes, boss,' Yellich said as Hennessey pulled up outside the Williamses' bungalow.

'Right. So that ties in with Lieutenant Williams's statement about getting home at about half past midnight, if Mr Vialli is correct about the time they left the Mill. Let's have a look inside the house.'

They left the car, ducked under the blue and white police tape which had been strung across the driveway from gatepost to gatepost and entered the house using the back door key.

'What are we looking for, boss?'

'Don't know, Yellich.' Hennessey turned the key in the lock. 'We'll know when we find it.' He opened the door and stepped over the threshold. 'Oh my . . .'

'What is it, boss?'

'Just the neatness, the tidiness, the everything-in-its-place-ness. I couldn't relax in this house. Little wonder the son was drawn to the navy. Anyway. If you wanted to find out about a woman's private life, where would you look?'

26

'The bedroom. Her dressing table.'

'So would I.'

'And if you wanted to find out about a man's private life, where would you look?'

'In his study if he has one; among his papers, at any rate.'

'So would I. Man does. Woman is. There is still much truth to that statement, despite what the angry sisterhood might think.'

'Yes, boss.'

'Right. We'll stay together. Bedroom first. Bit strong, isn't it? The smell of disinfectant, bleach as well, I think.'

'Just the sort of house it is, sir. And the windows haven't been opened much, in this heat, just the ideal conditions to make smells rise.'

'Daresay you're right. Let's find out about Mrs Williams.' Hennessey and Yellich went to the main bedroom of the house and slid between the bed and the dressing table, and Hennessey noted how there wasn't a seat in front of the dressing table. He said, 'She must have sat on the bed when putting on her war paint.'

'Must have, sir,' Yellich muttered, picking up a printed card from the table. 'But here's Sheringham.' He handed the card to Hennessey.

'Sheringham's Gym.' Hennessey turned the card over. It was blank on the reverse where he had noticed people often scribble messages of personal note. 'Holgate, York.'

'Nice and central,' Yellich offered. 'A lot of mixed housing there, plenty of old properties that could be turned into a gym.'

'We'll pay a call there.' Hennessey took a note of the address and then began to open the drawers of Mrs Williams's dressing table. In a deep drawer, at the back, behind expensive lingerie, was a small black notebook. It contained a series of entries, but one, 'Tim – the gym', and then the phone number of Sheringham's Gym, stood out. 'Tim Sheringham,' Hennessey mused. 'We ought to have a chat with him.'

'You know, boss, in the CID training course, they impressed

on us not to leap to conclusions, and not to dismiss the unlikely. That's what they said.'

'Did they indeed? Let's look at the study.'

Yellich turned and left the room. Hennessey followed.

'Yes, sir. They said that "improbable" and "impossible" are two different words, each with their own meaning, and CID officers shouldn't blur the meanings.'

'Don't say.' The two men stood in the living room of the house. 'I never actually did CID training. In my day, you were just promoted and you got on with it, learning as you went along.'

'The point being, that what is improbable is not impossible.'

'Well, there's wisdom for you.'

'Well, this is just a long-winded way of saying I think your waters are right. I thought it suspicious all along but I didn't dismiss kidnap or embezzlement.'

'Now you do?'

'Yes, boss.'

'We can still be wrong. I hope for Max and Amanda Williams's sake that we are. You said there was a study?'

'Here, sir. A little cubby hole with a bureau.'

Which Hennessey thought a very apt description. It was a small indentation off the dining room, which adjoined the living room; it had no door and contained just a modern, neat-looking, angular bureau, and a modern, upright chair, with the bureau having been pushed lengthways into the indentation and the chair wedged against it. He, like Yellich, noted that a person sitting on the chair had to place his or her legs at either side of it in order to be sitting at the bureau. Hennessey, feeling his joints to be too old for such acrobatics, stood beside the chair and lowered the bureau lid.

'Everything shipshape and Bristol fashion,' Yellich said, nothing the neatness of the papers in the bureau. 'Just like the rest of the house.'

'Everything what fashion?'

'Bristol fashion, boss. Mate of mine has a small yacht,

28

a twenty-five footer, keeps it in Hull Marina, uses that expression a lot.'

'Well, Bristol must be a neat town.'

'Don't know, boss. I've never been there.'

Hennessey threw him a pained look and then returned his attention to the contents of the bureau. He studied the Williamses' credit card statements. He gasped. The Williamses' credit limit was sufficient to buy a very good prestige second-hand car, maybe even a new car at the bottom end of the market. The balance outstanding was about the same amount. Against the 'payment received, thank you' the sum was modest in the extreme. Less than a meal for two in a good restaurant. 'Look at that, Yellich.' Yellich pondered the statements. 'He's been living at the edge of his credit. He's been spending money like . . .'

'Like there's no tomorrow. Apt, don't you think?'

'Double suicide, do you think, boss? Blow it all away then top themselves. It's not unknown.'

'Well, they've still got the bungalow . . . so all is not lost. But if they have been murdered, it wasn't for their money. And you were right to rule out kidnap and embezzlement. Nothing here to pay a ransom, nothing to embezzle. It veers me still further to the belief that the Williamses are no longer with us by the hand of A. N. Other, or others.'

The phone in the bungalow rang. Yellich and Hennessey looked at each other. Hennessey said, 'Better answer it.'

Yellich strode into the living room. He picked up the warbling phone and said, 'Hello . . . DS Yellich, North Yorkshire Police. Who is this? . . . Oh . . . right . . . well, no, we don't know what has happened to your parents. Can you hold the line, please?' Yellich pressed the monitor button on the phone and called to Hennessey. 'It's the daughter, sir, Nicola. She says she just heard from her brother and has phoned home. She says that there's no logic to her actions if her parents are missing, but she did it anyway on a whim. I can understand that, boss.'

'So can I, Yellich. Daresay I'd do the same if I was in her position. Right. Ask her when she last saw her parents, ask her if the name Sheringham, possibly Tim Sheringham, means anything to her, ask her if she knows of any enemies her parents might have and ask her for a contact phone number.'

'Right, sir.'

Hennessey listened as Yellich put the questions and the request to Nicola Williams. Yellich listened and then said, 'Yes, of course we'll let you know of any developments.' He replaced the phone and joined Hennessey in the dining room. 'Well, sir, she last saw her parents on Sunday. She said goodbye to both of them and drove to London. She confirms that her brother had left the house by then.'

'So she saw both of them. By the time she was ready to leave, her father had crawled groggily out of bed with a bad head.'

'It would appear so, sir. She left at about three p.m. That would be their last sighting. She knows Tim Sheringham.'

'She does?'

'Manager of the gym. Her mum goes to work out there, makes no secret of it.'

'She wouldn't if she was having an affair with the manager. Especially if said manager was younger than her son.'

'Aye, happen. She knows of no enemies that her parents might have. And she's given me her home and office phone number.'

'No known enemies.' Hennessey pondered. He picked up a statement of the Williamses' current account. 'Right at the limit of his credit and he'd be a rich man going by this statement were it not for the little "o/d" after the last figure. So money, as we've said, wasn't the motive. So it's got to be passion, negative passion, but passion nonetheless. And look at all these unpaid bills; I mean, how can someone get into this sort of debt and still take his family for a meal at the Mill?'

'Beats me, boss.'

'The sort of man for whom appearance is everything, that's who, Yellich. But you know, I don't know him, I don't know this man.'

'Williams?'

'Yes, Williams. I don't know him. You see, on the one hand he has this apparently repressive attitude to his house, which is quite cramped, everything-in-its-place exactitude. You'd think that was a man with his feet on the ground. Then, on the other hand, there's the Williams who's a fantasist, who's got this level of debt yet is treating his family to a meal with the most expensive wine in the best restaurant in the Vale of York, a man who is blissfully unconcerned about debt, the amount of which would have you and me on the point of suicidal despair. Those two personalities just don't go together. Not in my mind, anyway.'

'Well, you know what they say, sir?'

'No, what do they say?'

'There's nowt so queer as folk.'

'That's a gem of Yorkshire wisdom, is it?'

'Aye, well, they do say that.' Yellich felt a little uncomfortable. 'I mean, folk do such daft things that there's often no other explanation. It's like when you think you know someone and . . .'

'Yes. Thank you, Yellich, we'll save the homespun philosophy. I want to meet Tim Sheringham.'

Tim Sheringham revealed himself to be a well-built, muscular man whom both Hennessey and Yellich felt had a natural dislike for the police. He also appeared guarded, cautious, guilty. He sat in a cramped office, the window of which looked out onto a well-attended mixed gym of powerfully built men and svelte women in gaily-coloured gym strips. The rock tune 'Simply the best, Better than all the rest' pumped out of loudspeakers as the gym attendees pumped iron. Hennessey mused that often, before you can get people to do things you appeal to their vanity, and beyond Sheringham's office were about twenty people all at that point, putting a little extra effort in because they wanted to believe that they were simply the best, better than all the rest.

'Yeah,' Sheringham said, clean-shaven, crew-cutted, 'I knew her, so what?' He further revealed himself to speak in a curious blend of British English and American English, often, Hennessey believed, to be referred to as mid-Atlantic. Basically in this case it was British English with a smattering of American English words and turns of phrase and inflections. He had either lived for a while in the States or steeped himself in American films. Hennessey felt the latter; in his eyes Sheringham didn't look at all worldly wise.

'She's missing.'

Tim Sheringham paled.

'Hey, I haven't done anything.'

'Really?'

'Yes, really.'

'Nothing to worry about then, have you? When did you last see Mrs Williams?'

'Last week. Last Wednesday.'

'We understand you often see her on Wednesdays?'

'Maybe I do. Maybe I don't.'

'Maybe you'd just better tell us what you know.'

'About what? I've done nothing.'

'So you said. You're having an affair with Mrs Williams?'

'Look.' Sheringham hunched his shoulders. 'Just keep your voice down, will you?'

'Why? You bothered someone will hear?'

'Yes. I'm married. Mr Williams had some kind of golf club committee meeting on a Wednesday. So I went to her house on Wednesdays. We had to be discreet, he was a bit jealous.'

'Had. Went. Had. Was.'

'Sorry?'

'All past tense.'

'Yes.'

'As if he is deceased. And as if you know he's deceased.'

'Clever. But wrong. I broke it off with her. Last Wednesday I told her it was over. I'm married. It was fun, then it wasn't.'

'I see. Why did you start in the first place?'

'Mutual attraction.'

'Not many men in their twenties would find women in their mid-fifties attractive.'

'Nowt so queer as folk.'

'Funny you should say that, Mr Sheringham.'

'Oh?'

'Nothing. So how did it come about?'

'Because I'm physical. I'm very, very physical. For physical people the flesh is often very, very willing and the spirit is very, very weak. Yes, she was older than me, more than thirty years older. I was younger than her son . . . but I like cross-generational relationships. I get a thrill out of them. So did she.'

'Cross-generational relationships?'

'That's the term. You know, people who seek partners of different age groups, toy boys for the women, sugar mummys for the boys. I like it. She liked it. This is between you and me?'

'Of course.'

'I mean, if my wife were to find out . . .'

'She'd not be happy.'

'That would only be the beginning of it. Can't tell you what she'd do to me if she found out about me and Amanda. That's why I broke it off . . . the flesh was still willing, the spirit was still weak, but I got frightened of Vanessa.'

'Your wife?'

'Aye.'

'Where did you meet Mrs Williams?'

'Here in the gym.'

'How long ago.'

'About two years.'

'Long time ago, really.'

'Long enough. It was good for both of us. Like all affairs, it was better in the beginning, by last week all the fun had gone. It wasn't going anywhere and Vanessa . . .'

'You're frightened of your wife, you say?'

'What she can do. She could finish me. In the end the risk wasn't worth it. I mean, you'd be frightened of your wife finding out if your wife could do to you what my wife can do to me.'

'I'm not married.'

Sheringham sneered.

'Out of choice,' Hennessey said coldly.

'Of course.' Sheringham curled his lip. 'You've got to say that.'

'So how long have you been married?'

'About twelve months.'

'Twelve months!'

'That's what I said.' Sheringham looked pleased with himself.

'So you were having an affair throughout your engagement to your wife and for the first year of your marriage?'

'Yes,' Sheringham said smugly. 'Anything wrong with that? In fact, I met Amanda Williams before I met Vanessa. I ran them in parallel for about eighteen months.'

'In parallel. Is that how you see it?'

'That's just the way of it. A lot of women come in here to get in shape. I help them. I take them round the circuit. I take an interest in our clients.'

'Our?'

'My wife and I are partners in the gym.'

'Some you get to know better than others?'

Sheringham shrugged. 'Amanda had problems at home, her children were up and away, her husband drank like a fish . . . not giving her the attention a woman needs . . . she was in her fifties . . .'

'Was.'

'Is, then.'

'But you said "was".'

'Don't tie me up in knots.'

'Don't have to, Mr Sheringham, you're doing a good job of it yourself.'

Sheringham flushed with anger and gripped the arms of the chair he was sitting on. 'Don't say anything you might regret.'

'What's that supposed to mean?'

'Take it as you want to take it!'

'Got a temper, have you? Bet all those steroids don't help that.'

'Nothing I can't control.'

'Fortunate for you.'

'I want you out of my gym. I want you out now.'

'All in good time.'

'Now. Now!' Sheringham leaned forwards. 'I get what I want, when I want it and I want you two out of my gym now. I want you out. You have no choice.'

'You're right.' Hennessey nodded.

'So, go.'

'But if we go, you come with us.'

'And you come with us now,' Yellich said, slowly. 'Full gym or not.'

'On what charge?'

'Obstructing police enquiries. If we say you come with us, you come with us. *You* have no choice.'

A pause. Sheringham glared with anger.

'So,' Hennessey continued. 'You took up with Mrs Williams?'

'As I said.'

'And you saw her regularly until recently?'

'Yes.'

'And you broke it off?'

'Yes.'

'Because?'

'Because I was getting fed up, because I was frightened of my old lady . . . because, because.'

'How did she take it?'

'Like any mid-fifties dame would take it when her toy boy flies the coop. I won't be easy to replace in her life and she knew it.'

'Knew?'

'Knew, know, what does it matter?'

'Quite a lot. Were you bothered at all?'

'Some. She was loaded, meals at fancy restaurants, had an amazing house once . . . huge thing . . . the Grange . . . we'd play serious games there before Vanessa came on the scene . . . huge old house . . . she'd hide me away in a room where he never went and visit me secretly . . . he'd be in the house . . . kept me for a week once . . . that was fun.'

35

'Enjoy being kept, did you?'

'Yes. Anyway, they sold it, the Grange, and moved to the bungalow, easier to look after, she said. It was a bit of a comedown from the Grange but it was all right. I grew up in Tang Hall, so the bungalow was still good living. She said the sale of the Grange was a good move for her husband, released a lot of cash for his business ventures. So she said. But I wasn't interested in that. She was bored, she had her needs. A woman does.'

'And you helped out?'

'Yes. On Wednesdays. Wednesdays and Sundays are women-only days at the gym. They're my days off. Wednesdays were his committee day at the golf club. We'd meet at her bungalow . . . we'd do it late afternoon, early evening, then she'd take me for a meal, a good, or less good, restaurant depending on how she felt I had performed. It was our little game. I didn't always make it to the Mill. But occasionally I did. She set high standards. But that's the way to do it, you know. Sex on an empty stomach and no alcohol, then your meal in a restaurant. Do it the other way round, then it's not so good, too much food and wine dulls the sensation.'

'In your book?'

'It's good advice. Try it. I mean if you ever have the opportunity.'

'I'll remember that. So where's Mrs Williams?'

'I don't know. And I don't care.'

Hennessey drove home to Easingwold. He walked his garden with his dog, tail wagging, at his feet, happy to be out after a day-long confinement in the house. It was because of the garden that he had kept the house. His house itself was a modest three-bedroom detached property, set back from the Thirsk Road at the edge of the small town. A small lawn to the front, behind a high but neatly clipped hedge stood to the front of the house. It was at the rear of the house that Hennessey was most at ease, for here was a generous lawn, bounded by privet, and beyond, through a gap in the privet, was an orchard, with the trees planted in rows between paths made up of slabs of Yorkshire stone, and beyond the orchard was an area of waste ground, where a pond had been dug and in which pond life thrived, venturing distances which surprised Hennessey. Once, one evening, he returned home from walking Oscar and he and Oscar had turned into his drive and walked slowly behind a frog which was also clearly returning home, and while he and Oscar entered the house, the frog had been observed to traverse the lawn and enter the orchard, making its way to the pond in what Hennessey referred to as the 'going forth'. In the rear garden of his house, just he and Oscar, Hennessey knew tranquillity. Micklegate Bar Police Station might as well have been on another planet when he was in his back garden. That evening in June, after returning home, still feeling a little irritated by Tim Sheringham's personality, he ate a simple but wholesome casserole, took Oscar for a walk and then strolled into Easingwold for a Guinness at the Dove Inn.

3

Wednesday morning

. . . in which a lush pasture gives up its dead, a witness is revisited, and murder is confirmed.

Colin Less was a countryman. A son of the soil in any man's eyes. He had worked for the successive owners of Primrose Farm for thirty years. On the Wednesday of that week he went, spade in hand, as requested, in order to assess the state of the ditching. It was the first thing he did that morning, arriving there at about eight a.m. Yet by the time he arrived, the sun was high in the sky and the morning haze had long, long evaporated. He saw the mound of recently turned soil the instant he entered the five acre. He could not really have missed it. His immediate impression, drawing from his long years of experience on the land, was that whatever had been buried in the field had been buried very recently. His further impression was that whatever had been buried had only been buried shallowly: the mound of freshly tilled earth was too high, or 'proud' above the level of the field to be anything but a shallow burial. He would not know until he read the newspapers over the next few days, and then some months hence when he read the newspaper reports of a trial at York Crown Court, that his first impression was quite correct: it had been a recent burial. But he found out there and then that his second impression was also correct: it was a shallow burial. He had dug down only about one foot from the surface of the mound, to about six inches below the surface of the surrounding pasture when he struck an object. It was a human foot, still encased in a male shoe and sock and, so far as he could see, the leg to which it was still attached was encased in the trousers of an expensive-looking suit. Colin Less covered up the small hole he had excavated and walked to the nearest village where he knew stood a phone box outside the post office. He didn't rush the one-mile walk, but strolled, enjoying his fit, muscular body, enjoying a summer's morning in rural England. For he had reached the age in life where he knew that he was time limited, and often the reminders of mortality were about him, more so, much more so than a town dweller who takes his meat from a supermarket shelf. His discovery of human remains served only to bring the message about, not just the inevitability of death, but also its inescapability, home to him all the more clearly. So he savoured his life, and the richness and lushness of life about him, the foliage, the birdsong, the history of it and the certain continuance of it after his time. There was, after all, no hurry. Whoever the man was, he thought, he had already arrived where he was going. And his corpse wasn't going anywhere.

Hennessey followed the directions that he had been given and turned down a narrow lane between high hedgerows and reflected that in other circumstances he might have found the drive enjoyable. He came to a place where the lane ran between woodland and then the land opened out into flat fields, and it was there, where the woods gave way to the fields, that he saw the line of vehicles which marked his destination. There was an area car, still with its blue light revolving, a little unnecessarily, in Hennessey's view, a mortuary van, black, sombre, windowless, and further beyond, he saw Yellich's fawn-coloured Escort, and beyond that, to his delight, he saw a post-World War Two vintage Riley, white with red front mudguards and running boards. His son had once owned a die-cast toy model of such a vehicle, identical colour scheme as well. He halted his own car behind the mortuary van and walked to the entrance of the field, across which a blue and white police tape had been strung. Beyond the tape stood a group of people, one or two in uniform. One, not in uniform, held up a camera and photographed something on the ground. As Hennessey approached the tape the constable standing at the entrance to the field said, 'Good morning, sir,' and lifted the tape, allowing him to pass underneath it. Hennessey walked up and stood beside Yellich.

'Two adults, sir. One male, one female. Recently buried, as you see, clothing in place.'

'Well, hello, Mr and Mrs Williams.' Hennessey glanced at the corpses. 'We meet at last, I have heard so much about you.'

'That would be my inclination, sir.' Yellich smiled. 'I mean, as to their identity.'

'Yellich, you would sadden me to the point of clinical depression if that had not been your . . . inclination.'

'Yes, sir.' Yellich felt uncomfortable and glared at a constable who was beginning to, but did not actually, smile at his discomfort.

Hennessey glanced at the bodies. She was slender, light-coloured hair, angular facial features. He was tall, short dark hair, moustache, postmortem stubble. Both seemed to be expensively dressed. She, in her youth, would have considered herself and been considered a beauty: he likewise, handsome.

'Good morning, Chief Inspector.'

Hennessey turned. Dr D'Acre stood beside him. 'I've just been a few feet away to collect soil samples for comparative analysis, but I think this soil is not alien to the location. They were not buried elsewhere for safe keeping, exhumed and then reburied here.' She was, like Mrs Williams had been in life, slender, with close-cropped hair, large-framed, stainless-steel spectacles, boldly stating that she is a woman who wears spectacles and does not care at all. Not for her the vanity of contact lenses, nor, Hennessey doubted, when the time comes, would she be one for dentures. But perhaps she would. She was the same height as Hennessey, tall for a woman, he always thought.

40

'Dr D'Acre.' Hennessey smiled. 'I haven't seen you in a while.'

'Well, things have been quiet, criminally speaking,' she said. 'Plenty of PMs on deaths by misadventure, children drowning in the Ouse because it looks inviting on a hot summer's day, but no one has told them about undercurrents and eddies and stream flow; and farm workers trampled by bulls or impaled on agricultural machinery; elderly people who burn to death because their clothing catches fire. It all happens in the Vale, but little of recent note for the boys in blue. Mind you,' Louise D'Acre said with a smile, 'when we do get murders in the Vale, in North Yorkshire, they have a certain class about them, don't you think? I mean, grubby pit village stabbings on Saturday night belong to South Yorkshire, West Yorkshire has its share of senseless violence, but we in North Yorkshire, particularly in the Vale, have murders of class.'

'If you wish, Dr D'Acre, if you wish.' It had taken Hennessey some time to fathom Louise D'Acre's sense of humour, but when it had finally plumbed its depth he enjoyed, even envied, its dryness. 'But this is murder?'

'Oh, yes, I'd say so. Daresay you could commit suicide having arranged for a friend to bury you.'

'I was being serious.'

'So was I. Discounting possibilities, you see. They could have been killed accidentally and buried in a panic, by the motorist who ran into them while they were strolling down the lane and he was speeding whilst under the influence, but again, I don't think so. The police surgeon has pronounced life extinct. He did that at nine-thirty. Something of a formality in this case, but these things have to be done correctly.'

'Of course.'

'But is it murder?' The Home Office pathologist glanced at the two corpses, lying on their sides facing each other. 'It's not death by misadventure, it isn't suicide. It also isn't manslaughter followed by unlawful disposal of human remains. This is murder most foul. A man and a woman in their fifties, I'd say, both well-nourished, lived high on the hog,

41

I suspect. I mean, look at the clothing and the jewellery, and his wristwatch, that's a Cartier, isn't it?'

'Most probably, and they did live well.'

'You know them?'

'Well, professionally speaking . . . yes and no . . . never met them in life but we have known that they were missing, since Sunday last, but not reported until yesterday. I have every confidence that you're looking at the remains of Max and Amanda Williams, of Old Pond Road, Bramley on Ouse.'

'That's not too far from here. A pretty village. If it's the one I'm thinking of, magnificent yew in the churchyard. The church too is interesting, has ancient beams which look as though they've been bored by immense beetles, but not a bit of it, at the end of each hole there's a musket ball – a group of Cromwell's soldiers entered the church and blasted it from the inside with their muskets. Vandalism is no new thing.'

'Neither is graffiti. Beverley Minster has it from the six-teenth century.'

'That's recent. Take a trip to Rome. Anyway, I can at this stage observe nothing that contradicts the report that they were alive a few days ago. But what I can tell you is that they were not buried immediately.'

'Oh?'

Louise D'Acre nodded. 'Yes. They were buried about twenty-four hours after being killed.' She knelt by the shallow grave and took the forearm of the male corpse and bent it at the elbow. It moved quite freely. 'See that?'

'Yes.'

'There's no rigor mortis.' Louise D'Acre stood. 'You see, rigor begins to set in soon after death and in these climatic conditions, it will be fully established in twenty-four hours. Once the rigor has been broken it doesn't re-establish itself. So what happened is that they were murdered, then allowed to remain wherever for a period of at least twenty-four hours, then they were moved. But by the time they had to be moved, rigor had established itself and so to facilitate the removal of the corpses, the rigor had to be broken. You do that by forcing a joint to move. Takes a bit of strength to do that.

Then, once the rigor has been broken, you can bundle the body up into a compact place, possibly for transportation. I'll tell you more about the likely time of death once I get them to the pathology department.'

'Cause of death?'

'A blow to the head. More than one blow to the head of the man, just one to the woman that I can detect, but a blow to the head nonetheless. Both the scalps are matted with blood so there'll be traces of blood at the crime scene if the crime scene was indoors, less likely to trace blood if the crime scene was in the middle of a wood.'

'No trace of anything here, sir, except the grave. No tyre tracks, no footprints, the ground is concrete hard – it's been baked in the sun.'

'Who found the bodies?'

'A farm worker, sir. Gentleman by the name of Less.'

'Less?' Hennessey smiled.

'Aye, boss. So he says. Colin Less. Lives in a tied cottage on Primrose Farm land. This is Primrose Farm land.'

'I see.'

'He said he didn't see or hear anything of the grave being dug, but he knows the farm, he was in this field before the weekend, no trace of it then. But he says his experience would tell him that the grave was dug on Monday or yesterday.'

'I don't think I can do anything more here,' Dr D'Acre said. 'I'll have the bodies removed to York District. Who will represent the police at the PM?'

'Yellich, can you do that?'

'Yes, sir.'

Hennessey turned to D'Acre. 'Can I look in the pockets?'

'You can for me, Chief Inspector.'

Hennessey kneeled and felt the inside pocket of the man's jacket and extracted a wallet. He stood and opened it. 'Confirmation,' he said. 'As if we really needed it.' He showed it to Yellich.

'Max Williams,' Yellich read. 'Robbery wasn't the motive.'

Hennessey showed the wallet to D'Acre. 'A name for my report then.'

'Certainly looks like it.' Hennessey turned to Yellich. 'We've got some bad news to break.'

'I can do that, sir, collect the son from the naval base, ask him to formally identify the bodies. That'll have to be done before the postmortem.'

'Certainly will,' Louise D'Acre said. 'I'll have to peel the skin from the skull. His face won't be recognizable after I've finished. Neither will hers.'

Yellich and Louise D'Acre departed the scene separately. Hennessey remained at the scene to supervise the removal of the corpse. The corpse of Amanda Williams was last to be lifted from the shallow grave. As it was lifted clear, something shiny caught Hennessey's eye, it was on the bottom of the hole, having been covered by Amanda Williams's corpse. He knelt down and picked it up. It was a black ballpoint pen with a gold clip. One side was embossed with the words 'Sheringham's Gym – York'.

The Alert status was 'Bikini Red' when Yellich arrived at HMS Halley, so that on this occasion neither he nor his vehicle were allowed on the base. Lieutenant Williams, they said, would come to him.

Hennessey and two constables drove to the Williamses' bungalow in Old Pond Road, Bramley on Ouse. He noted that the drive between the shallow grave and the bungalow took just ten minutes. Leaving one of the constables at the entrance to the driveway, Hennessey and the second constable walked up the driveway and entered the garage. Hennessey fumbled for the key in the place it was usually kept.

It wasn't there.

He felt along the shelf. No key to be found. It had been removed. Displaced, at least. Followed by the constable, he walked round to the rear of the bungalow and peered into the back bedrooms. Then into the living room, then the dining room.

Disarray.

It was the only word he could think of to describe the

state of the interior of the once neat and just-so Williamses' bungalow. Ransacked, he then thought, might be another word. He turned to the constable. 'Check the door, will you, please.'

The constable did so. 'Unlocked, sir,' he said. He was, thought Hennessey, about nineteen, about the same age as the young lad with a machine pistol who had greeted him and Yellich when they had visited HMS Halley the previous afternoon.

Hennessey and the constable entered the bungalow cautiously. It appeared to him that everything had been disturbed. Yet there was a pattern to the chaos. He said so. 'This is not a burglary.'

'No, sir?'

'No, sir. Tell me why it's not a burglary?'

'It looks like a burglary to me, sir. I've seen houses in this sort of mess that have been burgled. Stuff flung everywhere . . .'

'Yes, I'm sure you have, but this is not a burglary.'

'I'd say it was, sir.'

'Then you'd be wrong.'

'I would, sir?'

'You would. You'd be wrong because items of value remain. That clock, for example. Go into the main bedroom at the front of the bungalow, tell me if a pile of cash is still on the dresser.'

The constable did so, returned and said, 'It's still there, sir.'

'You see, that cash and the clock and other items wouldn't have remained if this was a burglary. If this was mindless vandalism then there would be damage and the spraying of much paint. You've seen that sort of mess?'

'I have, sir.'

'What this is, Constable, is a ransacking. The person or persons who did this were looking for something. And it was done by the person or persons who knew where the Williamses kept their back door key hidden.' Hennessey took his mobile phone from his jacket pocket, switched it on and pressed a ten-figure number. The constable standing close to

Hennessey heard the full, high-pitched, crackly exchange.

'Yellich.'

'Hennessey. Where are you?'

'Outside the naval base. They're fetching Lieutenant Williams for me.'

'Right. Listen. When you've done the identification, take him to Micklegate Bar and put him in an interview room.'

'Why, sir? He's not a suspect, is he?'

'No, he's not, but someone has ransacked his parents' house, as if looking for something. He might know who'd want to do that, or what they were looking for.'

'Very good, sir. Do you want me to tell him that as soon as I can?'

'Why not? Give him a chance to think. How long do you think you'll be?'

'Can't really . . . hang on, this looks like him now, Land Rover's approaching the gate at a rate of knots, officer in the front passenger seat . . . yes, this is Williams now.'

'Right. I'll see you back at Micklegate Bar.' Hennessey switched off the mobile phone. 'Right, lad.'

'Sir?'

'Someone looked for something. That means one of two things.'

'He or she or they found it or they didn't?'

'Good. What do we do first?'

'Look for it ourselves, sir?'

'No. This is now a crime scene. If it wasn't before, it now is. We need Scene of Crimes down here, get this photographed and dusted for prints. Then we'll talk to the neighbours, see if they saw anything.' He took his mobile phone from his pocket and dialled Micklegate Bar Police Station. 'You go and join your mate at the bottom of the drive.'

'Yes, sir.'

'No one enters the property unless it's the police.'

'Very good, sir.'

Yellich drove at a steady pace from HMS Halley to the York District Hospital on Wiggington Road. Initially the two men sat in silence, but as soon as they had cleared Knaresborough and were once again driving through open country, Yellich said, 'I'm afraid that I have to tell you, sir, that we have every reason to believe that you'll be making a positive identification.'

'You believe so?'

'Yes, sir. I'm very sorry. We found a wallet on the person of the deceased male. It had your father's name and address.'

'Oh . . .' The man seemed distant, hardly surprising, thought Yellich . . . in any man's language, this is a milestone in his life. Then Williams said. 'The little cretin.'

'Sir?' Yellich turned to Williams and saw then that the man wasn't in a state of shock at all, his silence was caused by his being in a state of anger, jaw set hard as if burning up with resentment.

'I said, the little cretin.'

'Who, sir, not your father surely?'

'No . . . not my father . . . I'm sorry for him . . . I want to help you as much as I can . . . but I meant that bloody able seaman. You might have seen him on the platform outside the provost marshal's office.'

'We did, sir.'

'He went absent without leave. Went home because his mother was ill. Commander fined him three days' pay. Me, I would have strung the cretin up from the yardarm. I mean, what would happen to the Queen's Navy if we all went home every time mummy sneezed? Tell me that.'

'Yes, sir. Did you hear what I said about the likelihood of you making a positive ID in a few minutes' time?'

'Yes. I heard. You found my father's wallet.'

'You don't seem to be bothered.'

'Why should I be? What's done is done. It's the living that matter. And naval discipline . . . that cretin went away chuckling with his mates . . . I'll get him for something. Don't you worry about that. No one gets the better of me.'

Yellich stared at the road ahead of him. 'We don't believe that money was the motive for your parents' murder . . . there was cash in the house, and your father's watch . . .

47

if it is your father . . . his watch was on his wrist . . . it's a Cartier.'

'I know.'

'And, like I said, his wallet was in his jacket pocket, had a bit of money in it, plus his credit cards . . .'

'So what was the motivation?'

'That's what we were hoping you'd help us with.' Yellich was pleased that Williams was now focusing on the murder, rather than a hapless young able seaman. He feared for the welfare of any young serviceman whose officer had 'got it in for him'. 'You see, there's something else I have to tell you, sir, and that is that your parents' house has been ransacked.'

'Ransacked! The village lads have got in.'

'No . . . someone let themselves in, and appeared to be searching for something.'

'Really? What?'

'Well, that's the question I was going to ask you, sir. Do you know who would want what from your parents' house?'

'I don't really.'

'We found a ballpoint pen where the deceased were buried, had "Sheringham's Gym" embossed on it.'

'My mother went to the gym to work out. She wanted to keep her figure as long as she could. The gym gave the pens out as freebies some time ago, promotional gimmicks. My mother used the pen, but only in the home . . . wouldn't be seen dead . . . sorry . . . didn't want to be seen writing cheques with it, but in the home was acceptable in her eyes.'

'We were hoping it might mean something.'

'I don't think it does. But that cretin better have a guardian angel.'

The rest of the journey was passed in silence. Stressful, tense, silence.

In the mortuary of York District Hospital, Yellich and Williams sat on a bench in a softly lit, silent room, a velvet curtain hung over one wall. A door opened and a nurse came in and with an attitude of sorrow and solemnity, held a cord by the side of the curtain.

'It will not be as you have seen in the films,' Yellich said. 'If you'd like to stand in front of the curtain.'

Williams nodded. Yellich in turn nodded to the nurse when he and Williams stood side by side in front of the curtain. The nurse then pulled the cord and the curtain opened in complete silence. The dead man lay on a trolley in a darkened room. His head was neatly and tightly bound with bandage, the sheets were neatly and firmly tucked in, so that viewing the body through the mirror, by some trick of light and shade, he appeared to be floating in space.

'That,' Williams said, 'is my father.'

'Thank you, sir.' Yellich nodded to the nurse and the curtain slid shut. The nurse exited by the door through which she had entered and moments later returned to the room. She glanced at Yellich, who nodded, and the curtain was once again opened.

'And that,' Williams said. 'That is my mother.'

'Back again?' Thom stood outside his house, the front door was open and Thom's dog sat in the hall of the house, keeping himself out of the sun, though he eyed Hennessey cautiously as he walked up the drive.

'Back again?' Hennessey smiled.

'You are the police. I can see two constables at the Williamses' bungalow and you have that stamp about you. I can tell police officers, with or without a uniform.'

'Sorry it shows.' Hennessey approached the man.

'Oh, it shows.'

'And you are?'

'Edward Thom, schoolmaster, retired.'

'Ah . . . yes. It was you who first raised concern. I remember your name in the report. I'm Hennessey, Chief Inspector.'

Thom nodded at the tall, gaunt-looking man, a man in his mid- to late-fifties, a man of eyes which, thought Thom, showed both wounding and wisdom.

'Mr Thom, did you see or hear anything suspicious last night? That is, anything of that nature in respect of the Williamses' bungalow.'

'Yes. Yes, I did as a matter of fact. Heard more than saw, in fact heard rather than saw, didn't see anything at all.'

'Oh?'

'Heard a car in the lane, a powerful-sounding car, thought at first it was the Williamses' son checking the house, but it wasn't his car. He has a sports car but I've heard his car often enough to recognize it. This car had an engine which had a much deeper note, a very powerful machine. Came at about midnight, we'd just returned from our walk, me and my best friend in there . . .'

Hennessey smiled. 'I have a dog. I understand the relationship.'

'What sort?'

'Mongrel.'

'Good . . . anyway, I heard the car arrive and I heard it drive away again at about one a.m.'

'But you didn't see anything?'

'I did not, Mr Hennessey, but I did see something about a week ago. It actually didn't occur to me when I spoke to the constable yesterday morning, but now I may be seeing the awful significance of it. But it's only significant if a tragedy has befallen the Williamses. If they turn up safe and well, then what I saw cannot be relevant.'

Hennessey paused. 'Well, Mr Thom, without divulging details, I can tell you, off the record, that a tragedy has befallen the Williamses, that ours and your worst fears are confirmed.'

'Oh . . .' Thom groaned. 'I am sorry. Well, in that case, on Thursday of last week I heard a man threaten to kill the Williamses, Mr Williams particularly.'

'You heard someone threaten to kill the Williamses?'

'Heard and saw,' Thom said. 'You can see for yourself that the Williamses' driveway is visible from where we are standing, you can see it through the trees.'

'Yes.' Hennessey nodded in agreement. 'It's a clear enough sight.'

'And it's a good acoustic pocket as well,' said Thom. 'Your constable there will be hearing our conversation quite audibly.'

50

'Really?'

'Yes, really. Call to him in a normal voice . . .' Hennessey did so, not raising his voice any, he said, 'Constable, can you hear me?'

'Yes, sir,' the constable replied. 'Clear as a bell.'

'My heavens.' Hennessey was genuinely surprised.

'It isn't just a function of the silence, so that your voice has nothing to compete with, it's a function of that wall there.' Thom pointed across Old Pond Lane to the slab-sided brick wall of a detached house which stood opposite and between Thom's house and the Williamses' bungalow. 'Talking to your constable just now was like bouncing a snooker ball off the cushion. If it hits the cushion at forty degrees it'll bounce off at forty degrees. Your voice and the constable's answer did not directly travel between you, it travelled across the lane, bounced off the wall of that house and travelled back across the lane.'

'Astounding.'

'Elementary, actually,' said Thom. 'But that explains how I heard as well as saw what happened on Thursday.'

'Which was?'

'Fellow called Richardson. Irish by his accent, despite his English name . . .'

'Well, I'm English with an Irish name.'

'Point taken . . . He had a length of scaffolding in his hand, waving it about his head, the Williamses were backed up against their door . . . he was threatening to brain them, they threatened him with the police. He said, "Go on, call them, you're the criminals, not me."'

'He had a scaffolding pole in his hand?'

'Not a twenty-one.'

'A what?'

'A twenty-one. Full-length scaffolding poles are known as "twenty-ones" in the building trade because they're that long measured in feet. I had an extension built on my house a year or two ago and I was chatting to the builders and I picked up that piece of information. When a scaffolding pole is bent it can't properly be straightened and so the straight bits are cut

51

off and make handy short bits to put at the end of gangways and suchlike.'

'And this fellow had one such short bit?'

'Yes, about two feet long. He was a big man, hands like bears' paws, well able to grip a scaffolding pole. Anyway, the thing didn't escalate into violence and the angry Irishman drove away in a small lorry – I think they're called pick-ups – which had "Richardson – Builders" painted on the side of the door. I am just assuming that the angry Irishman was Mr Richardson.'

'Do you know what the row was about?'

'Money. Richardson said that if he didn't get his money then Williams's blood would be spilled, and if she got in the way, she'd get it too. I assume "she" was a reference to Mrs Williams. Charming fellow.'

'It's a fair assumption, I'd say.' Hennessey looked at the house which stood on the other side of the lane, on the wall of which voices had bounced between Thom's house and the Williamses' house. 'I wonder if the people who live in that house saw anything?'

'Plenty, I expect. He's a vet, recently retired and celebrating the fact by taking his wife on a world cruise with Cunard. Daresay they'll be somewhere between Sydney and San Francisco right now.'

Hennessey chuckled.

'Reinforcements?' Thom said, as a white van slowed to a stop outside the Williamses' bungalow.

'Scene of Crimes Officers.'

'The Williamses' bungalow is a scene of a crime, then?'

'Yes. Now it is.'

'And I came here for a quite retirement.'

'That will be my findings, Sergeant Yellich.' Louise D'Acre removed the gauze mask from her mouth and pondered the bodies, laying side by side on twin stainless-steel tables, the top of the skull of each having been removed, thus exposing the brain. 'Both died of head injuries, but both died differently.'

'What was that term you used . . . for him, Dr D'Acre?'

'For him, he died of a subarachnoid haemorrhage. What happened to him is that he sustained multiple blows to the head but he has quite a thick skull. His skull didn't fracture at all, but the blows caused subcranial lacerations and the blood collected in the subarachnoid space. What happened then is that the blood was prevented from coagulating because it mixed with the cerebrospinal fluid which dilutes it and it then slides down inside the skull to cover the brain and enter the basal skull fossae, and death follows.' She peeled off her latex gloves from her hands. 'The process is not fully understood, but when the brain stem comes into contact with blood, death occurs.'

The mortuary assistant covered the bodies with sheets.

'Thank you, Mr Filey.' D'Acre smiled at the small bespectacled man, who smiled his acknowledgement. 'The fact that he had been drinking, he has a high blood/alcohol level, the alcohol would have eased the bursting of aneurisms, the blood vessels.'

'I see.'

'So that is he. Now she, on the other hand, did suffer a fractured skull. A single blow cracked her skull open from front to back, sending brain splinters into the skull, killing her instantly. A blunt instrument was used in both cases.'

'Time of death?'

'Found this morning . . . I noted a slight discolouration of the abdominal skin, that is the usual sign for the onset of putrefaction, which normally takes place within two to three days after death. They probably were not killed last night, probably any time from Sunday to Monday evening . . . but they would have been deceased by yesterday morning. I think of interest to you is the hypostasis, that was the redness about the buttocks, the shoulders and the calves and ankles.'

'I remember.'

'That fully established itself in six to twelve hours after death and is basically a settling of blood in the body due to gravity, especially where the body has been exposed to a cold surface. When they had died, they were both laid on the ground face up and remained there for about twenty-four hours, during which rigor mortis set in. Then they were moved, the rigor was broken, and they were then taken to the shallow grave and placed on their sides. If they had been buried soon after death in the manner in which they were found, then rigor would be present and the hypostasis would be present down one or the other side, not on the posterior aspect of their bodies.'

'Moved after death,' Yellich said. 'Alive on Sunday, deceased by Tuesday, moved after death.'

'They were probably buried on the Tuesday evening, that is yesterday and today's hours of darkness. Found this on her clothes.' D'Acre held a small glass test tube and handed it to Yellich.

'A butterfly?'

'A moth.' D'Acre looked at the test tube. 'What great monument of purpose you were destined for and never knew it, eh, little one? You see, Sergeant, it's my guess that in the burial of the two bodies in a shallow grave, there would be a lot of movement, bodies being carried and dumped, soil being heaved . . . would there not?'

'Yes, I would imagine so.'

'It's my further guess that this wee beastie – it's a common moth, nothing out of the ordinary about it – came fluttering along, possibly attracted by a light from a lantern or car headlights, and by some means got caught up in the movements, had a spadeful of soil chucked over him. Got in the way of a spadeful of soil, was brought down as he fluttered by, didn't recover before the next spadeful of soil landed on him and his goose was cooked. But his presence meant that he was in the vicinity at the time of the burial, that means it was a night burial. Allowing for time for rigor to establish itself, because it was broken, then they could not have been buried Monday night/Tuesday morning, they had to have been buried last night. And murdered at least twelve hours before that.'

'So . . . they were seen alive on Sunday in the afternoon . . .'

'Any time from then until yesterday morning was the time

of their death, if you're certain they were alive on Sunday afternoon.'

'Their children saw and spoke with them.'

'Good enough, I suppose, but clinically speaking, I'd be prepared to push the time envelope back twenty-four hours, but that's at the extreme. If you think that the witnesses to their being alive on Sunday are reliable, then that would fit with my clinical findings that death was likely to have occurred between' – she glanced at the clock on the wall – 'between about twenty-four and fifty-two hours ago.'

'Between Sunday night and Tuesday morning?'

'If you like, but I can narrow it down further.'

'You can?'

'Stomach contents reveal a partially digested heavy meal.'

'They were known to have been at a restaurant on Saturday evening, returning home about midnight.'

'Well, it takes about twenty-four hours for a meal to be digested and the waste vacated per rectum and heavy, fatty meals remain longer than light meals, as you'd expect, and digestion does continue after death. But the presence of the Saturday-evening meal in their system points to death nearer to the fifty hours end of the time window.'

'Closer to the Sunday?'

'Yes. Much closer to the Sunday.'

'She didn't say what sort of weapon was used, boss,' Yellich said in Hennessey's office. 'Apart from a blunt instrument.'

'Plenty of those. Do you think it could be a scaffolding pole, that it to say a short length of same?'

'Have to ask her that, boss.'

'I will.' Then, by means of explanation Hennessey told Yellich about Richardson, his visit to the Williamses', his threat and the two-foot-long length of scaffolding pole. 'What did Williams say about anybody wanting to murder his parents?'

'Not a lot. He's a queer fish, boss, no mistake. You'd think he'd be upset about going to identify his parents, but on the journey he was obsessed by that sailor.'

'What sailor?'

'The lad on the platform outside the provost marshal's office.'

'Oh yes,' Hennessey spoke softly. 'I did wonder what his story was.'

Yellich told him.

'Seemed to take it personally, then?'

'Seemed so.'

'What about his reaction when he saw his parents' bodies?'

'That was more natural. A bit restrained, but sorrowful, subdued. Daresay he is a human being after all.'

When Yellich had gone, Hennessey suddenly remembered another name: Bestwood. Bestwood, that's another name for the list, one perfunctory, lacklustre, flat-personality lump of a lad, he, little wonder he hadn't been one of the first to spring to mind. But that's another name for the list, but he was betting there. He was confident that soon he'd have all thirty-two names. He couldn't remember Bestwood's Christian name though. He thought it was probably Michael, but only probably.

4

Wednesday afternoon and evening

. . . in which Chief Inspector Hennessey meets a ruined man, is annoyed and impressed by a scientist, and both he and Sergeant Yellich each make their favourite journey: home.

Rufus Williams sat impassively in the interview room. Hennessey was puzzled by his calmness, but then, he thought, then this was probably his way of reacting to misfortune, a state of denial, he believed it to be called – 'it's not really happening, it isn't really, it'll sort itself out, he's not really dead, it just looks that way.'

'Would you like us to contact the Metropolitan Police to ask them to break the news to your sister?'

'No. I'll do that. Thanks, anyway.'

'As you wish. We only have to inform one next of kin. The rest is up to the family.'

'I am aware of that.'

'Difficult as it must be for you, sir,' Hennessey pressed forward. 'I'm afraid we have to ask you some questions.'

'Of course.'

'This has now officially become a murder enquiry, a double murder enquiry, and so we must ask you not to go near your parents' bungalow. It's become a crime scene.'

'So they were murdered at home?'

'We don't know that. It's been ransacked and for that reason alone we have declared it a crime scene. We've still to establish the location of the murders. For all we know there may be two different locations.'

'How did they die?'

'Beaten about the head with a blunt instrument.'

Williams shook his head slowly. 'There's something unreal about this.' Hennessey nodded. This, he thought, was more like a normal reaction, more natural, more appropriate than the reaction that Yellich had reported: the obsession with the young able seaman, that was a clear denial reaction. 'One thing we are certain of is that your parents were not robbed. Money was not the motive.'

'I could have told you that. They have no money. None at all.' Williams looked Hennessey square in the eye. 'No money at all.'

'So it's fair to say that no one would benefit from their death, financially speaking?'

'That's fair.'

'Not even you and your sister . . . I mean the bungalow, any insurance policies . . .'

'If anything, it will be scraps. I don't know the extent of his bank accounts or building society accounts, if any, nor of his insurance policies. If any. The death certificate will only have been issued today. I've got to start wrapping up his estate . . . I just don't have the information you want but I suspect that if he left anything, it will be only enough to pay for his funeral.'

'What about the bungalow?'

'What about it?'

'It must be worth something?'

'It is, but not to us. So I believe, anyway. I don't know the extent of it but I suspect that Father had borrowed money from the bank, using the bungalow as collateral. He had been unable to repay the loan. So I believe, anyway.'

'All right. So neither your sister nor you would benefit from the death of your parents?'

'No.'

'Mr . . .'

'Lieutenant.'

'Lieutenant Williams, your parents were beaten about the head, that's passion. They were buried in a shallow grave, that's absence of premeditation. Who do you know, would have such feelings for your parents that they would want to kill them in such a violent way? Their murder was one of suddenly unleashed rage.'

'You've asked me this before and I still can't bring anyone to mind who would want to do that.' Williams shrugged. 'I'm sorry. But then again, he was a businessman . . .'

'And businessmen make enemies. I know.'

'Mother did once tell of a spat with a fellow called Richardson.'

'Oh yes?'

'Irishman, has a temper. So she said.'

'Tell me about him.'

'Don't know about him, but apparently Father had let him down in some way. I don't know the details, but Richardson felt he'd been let down by Father and was in a bad financial way because of it. You'll have to ask Richardson.'

'We will. He's a builder, isn't he?'

'I believe so.'

'Your father . . . you said he helped you financially?'

Williams scowled. Then he said 'Well, yes.'

'To a great extent?'

'That's relative. He helped me keep away from poverty. I could enjoy the social life of a naval officer without worrying too much.'

'I see,' Hennessey said. 'What will you do now?'

'What do you mean?'

'Well, from what you've told me, you're now dependent upon your salary and that can't be much.'

'Confess I haven't thought too much about it. I've a little in the bank. That's a useful cushion, but it won't last forever. Looks like civvy street for me, as I've said before. Maybe that's not a bad thing, I'm not going anywhere in the navy.'

'Confess, I thought you were a bit old for your rank.'

Williams's eyes narrowed.

'Always been in the navy?'

'Since I was seventeen.'

'Sea service?

'Yes. Of course.'

'But you don't wear spectacles?'

'Meaning?'

'Well, meaning that I did my National Service in the Andrew.'

'And?'

'Well, I did my tour, I saw the world as far as Portsmouth, but I came away with the impression that shore-based personnel are seen as second-raters by the sea service personnel.'

'That attitude exists.'

'It is also my experience that shore-based personnel had some medical problem that prevented them serving at sea, most wore spectacles, for example.'

'I fail to see your point.'

'Frankly, I don't know what the point is myself . . . but something doesn't add up.'

'Will that be all, Chief Inspector? I've got responsibilities to attend to, both family and professional.'

'Yes . . .' Hennessey stood. 'Sorry to have detained you.'

'Neither breakfast nor lunch.' Hennessey swallowed the coffee in his mug.

'Sorry, sir?' Yellich sat opposite him.

'The Williamses didn't have anything to eat after their meal at the Mill. That was their last meal in life.'

'Yes, sir.'

'Yet they were seen on the Sunday afternoon, so they forewent breakfast and lunch.'

'Not difficult to see why, boss. I mean, if they had pushed the boat out as much as the restaurateur said they had then they'd probably want nothing all day Sunday except coffee, endless mugs of same. Then maybe a cheese sandwich in the evening.'

'Fair point, so we don't go down that alley. The bug that Dr D'Acre found on Mrs Williams's clothing, in amongst the soil, was it?'

'Yes, sir, she said it could have been caught in a shovelful of flying soil as it fluttered by.'

'It was a moth. So it means they were buried at night.'

'Yes, sir.'

'Specifically last night.'

'Right. So we have the time window that Dr D'Acre proposes. From Sunday morning to this morning, specifically the hours of darkness of last night which is when she believes the Williamses were buried?'

'Yes, boss.'

Hennessey paused. 'Fifty-four cubic feet.'

'Boss?'

'A grave six feet long and three feet wide and three feet deep is fifty-four cubic feet. And that's fifty-four cubic feet of clay. This is the Vale of York, remember. Even in my prime I couldn't dig that sort of hole in six hours, which is the amount of darkness there was last night. So who's on the scene with a physique that could enable him to shift fifty-four cubic feet of clay in six hours? Clay that's been baked hard, to boot?'

'Tim Sheringham, for one.'

'And maybe Richardson, who Williams mentioned. Builders are not usually small guys. I think I'd like to meet Richardson. Particularly since Mr Thom, the neighbour, also mentions him.'

'There's another reason you'll want to meet Richardson, boss.'

'There is?' Hennessey's eyes widened.

'The name rang bells with me, did a little digging.'

'Digging,' Hennessey echoed. 'Apt in this case.'

Yellich smiled. 'Isn't it? But two years ago, a man in a field, left with his brains sticking out as though his head had been fed into a meat grinder. Solemn business.'

'Yes . . . now that you mention it. Fellow by the name of Kerr.'

'That's it, boss, Thomas "Toddy" Kerr, a large man, hence the nickname. A bit like calling a Great Dane "Tiny". I have the file here.' Yellich patted a file.

'Just remind me.'

'Well, it's one of the great unsolved in the Famous and Faire. Toddy Kerr owed a lot of money to a lot of folk and

61

we believed that one of them collected in kind rather than in cash, one of the debtors was . . .'

'Michael Richardson.' Hennessey beamed at Yellich. 'And, if I recall, he was the only one who didn't offer an alibi, left the burden of proof with us. A bit similar, don't you think?'

'Very similar, I'd say, boss. Solemnly so, in fact. And you say Mr Thom mentions him?'

Hennessey told him of Thom's information. Then he said, 'Do you know why builders call scaffolding poles "twenty-ones"?' Yellich confessed he didn't, so Hennessey told him that as well.

A lizard.

It was the only word that came to Hennessey as he sat opposite Michael 'Galway Mick' Richardson and pondered the over-wide mouth and bulging eyes and leathery skin, sitting with knees together beneath a huge frame and broad head and shoulders, so that his legs resembled a tail. It was not dissimilar to looking at children's books in which animals inhabited human surroundings. Here a lizard sat in a swivel chair in a cramped office. Richardson's tumbling, black curly hair and confident I-like-myself attitude also told Hennessey that here was a man who most probably enjoyed success with women.

'Yes. I knew Williams. I don't deny it. Why should I deny it? And now he's deceased.'

'You know that?'

'Lunchtime news.' Richardson nodded to the small radio on his desk.

Hennessey read the room. It was Richardson's office in his house on the edge of Overton. Very strong, very substantial, very ordered. A portable TV on a shelf at eye level if sitting at the desk. A builder's house.

'What exactly was your relationship with Mr Williams?'

'Didn't have one. Not at the end.'

'The reason I ask is that we have a very reliable witness who tells us that you threatened to kill him.'

'So?'

'Did you?'

'Yes, I did.'

Hennessey paused. 'You killed him?'

'No. I threatened to.' He had a soft-spoken manner.

'Oh.'

'Disappoint you?' Richardson smiled.

'No . . . no, I've been a policeman long enough to know that nothing is that easy.' Hennessey relaxed in the easy chair at the side of Richardson's desk. 'Tell me about the argument you had with him at his front door, last week, I believe.'

'He owes me money. He owes me a lot of money. An awful lot of money, so he does now. I've had to pay labourers, I've had to pay my skilled men. I need the money owed to me. It's called cash flow.'

'How much money are we talking about?'

'Enough.'

'How much is enough?'

'Enough to finish me. Six figures. That's enough. See, if I build a brick rabbit hutch and the fella doesn't pay I can survive, if I build a garage and the fella doesn't pay I may be able to survive. But if I build a house and the fella doesn't pay then I have a problem. And I don't just mean any house, I mean a four-bedroom detached house, bay windows, jacuzzi, double garage, fancy fittings in the bathroom . . . primed, papered, ready to move in. Even gave him the keys so he could start measuring up for carpets. He put the carpets in, paid for that. They've been living there to guard the place, there's a double mattress in the upstairs room, a duvet, some food in a small fridge, a few plates, electric kettle . . . she mainly, the clothes in the bin liner are all female . . . so I build the house to the plans he has had drawn up and then I say . . . OK, now pay me. So he says, "When I've sold it I will."'

'Oh.'

'I thought all along that it was for him to move into . . . he's known in the Vale . . . he's a man with money . . . a venture capitalist and he likes throwing it around. So I thought I was safe. Any other guy I'd want money upfront, or lodged with a solicitor to be retained on satisfactory completion . . . my error . . . he paid twenty thousand upfront, but that still leaves me with a shortfall of six figures.' Richardson's voice hardened. 'So, it's a breach of contract or something. It's unlawful.'

'It's not criminal,' Hennessey replied softly.

'There's two things I can do. I can pursue him through the civil courts, but that won't get me anywhere but a hefty legal bill because I built it on an assumption. So you built it on an assumption, so you're wrong, it's possibly not breach of contract. The other thing I can do is what I'm going to do, which is sell it. Technically speaking, it's my house, so I can sell it. But the house market is depressed, nothing is moving. It'll be at least eighteen months before anybody shows an interest. If I sell it quickly it'll be only because I've reduced the price so much that I'll be selling at a loss. He betrayed me. He was clearly hoping to sell it, pay me off and pocket the balance. But all along he let me believe he was going to move his family in.'

'So you went round to his house and threatened to kill him and his wife with a scaffolding pole.'

'Yes, I did. Wouldn't you?'

'No, I wouldn't. That length of scaffolding, where is it?'

'God knows.'

'I'm sure He does, but do you?'

'No. Maybe in the back of the truck.'

'I'd like to take it with me.'

'Help yourself, there's about half a dozen bits of scaffolding. I don't know which one I picked up.'

'Handy length, though, about two feet.'

'Handy?'

'To batter someone's head in.'

'Suppose it is. I've never done it.'

'No?'

'No.'

'This will finish you, you believe?'

'It will. I've built the business up from scratch. I've got a couple of small jobs on the go, but the brickies will need paying . . . I've got no cash to pay them, the bank won't advance me any . . . do you know what brickies do if they don't get paid?'

'Wreck the site?'

'They don't need to do that, they just take a sledgehammer and knock the bricks out of line six inches above the ground. Makes the whole structure invalid, won't pass Building Control Inspection. Can't sell it, have to demolish it. That's worse because you have to pay for the demolition. You know, if they wrecked the site they'd actually be doing me a favour.'

'Save the demolition cost?'

'Yes. It's the sort of thing that'd drive a saint mad, so it would.'

'It's the sort of thing that would make you want to kill someone.'

'It is that.'

'So did you?'

'What?'

'Kill them.'

'That's not funny.'

'It isn't. It isn't funny at all. Where were you last Sunday?'

'I don't know. Here. All day. At home. I have Sunday at home.'

'Anybody vouch for that?'

'No.'

'Live alone?'

'Me and my wife. Our children are up and away.'

'Your wife wasn't here on Sunday?'

'She was in Ireland. She came back this morning.'

'So you were in all Sunday?'

'I went to Mass at ten o'clock. I was in all Sunday after that.'

'What about Monday night?'

'What about it?'

'Where were you?'

'Here.'

'All night?'

'All night.'

'And Tuesday, last night?'

'Same. Stayed in alone, watching the TV so I did.'

'I see.'

'What does that mean?'

'Nothing. How long have you been in the building trade?'

'I'm forty-nine. I dug my first hole when I was fourteen. You work it out, I was never any good with numbers.'

'A long time.'

'Long enough. Never done anything else.'

'Ever been in trouble with the police?'

'Few times. I came over here as a labourer. When a bunch of labourers have had enough stout . . . you must have seen the results . . . being a copper, like.'

'Convictions for violence, then.'

'Yes. When I was a youngester. I calmed down once I got married. Calmed down more once I started out on my own.'

'So we'll have a record of you?'

'Nothing you can use in court. They're all spent now, my convictions, they're all spent.'

'But your fingerprints will be on file.'

'Reckon they will.'

'Tell me about Mr Kerr. Thomas "Toddy" Kerr.'

'What about him?'

'Did you kill him too?'

'I didn't kill anybody.' Said with controlled temper.

'Look at it from our point of view, "Toddy" Kerr owed you money.'

'He owed a lot of people, and he didn't owe me anything like what Williams owed me.'

'But he owed you, and his brains got beaten out of his skull with an instrument that would not be dissimilar to a short length of scaffolding.' Hennessey paused, but Richardson didn't react. 'And you couldn't offer an alibi.'

'So?'

'Well, Williams owed you money, you were seen and heard to threaten him with a short length of scaffolding and shortly afterwards his brains were beaten out of his head, and you have no alibi for the time the murder is believed to have taken place.'

'That's because I don't need one, for either murder.'

'Can't ignore the coincidence, though.'

'Can't convict on coincidence, though.'

'And you know that. Puts you in the frame, puts you well in the frame. You're always around when people get their brains removed forcibly from the inside of their head.'

'Where else would you remove them from?'

'Point to you.' Hennessey inclined his head, but Richardson was talking, and in situations like this Hennessey had often found that people trip themselves up. 'But you see our point?'

'I see no point at all, Chief Inspector. Especially since you're forgetting one thing. You're forgetting that if you kill someone you'll definitely not get your money back.'

'Perhaps you didn't consider that when your temper was well up.'

'I didn't consider it because I didn't kill them. I didn't kill Williams and his wife and I didn't kill Kerr. Felt like it, but that's not a crime. Besides which, Kerr wasn't buried, he was left out in the open, the Williamses were buried.'

'A minor difference. The main point is that you have the motivation in both cases, you have the passion that was required in both cases, and you have the physical strength to carry out both murders, and you have the strength to dig the shallow grave.'

'I didn't kill them, or Kerr.'

'Let me pick your brains.'

'I didn't know Englishmen believed the Irish had brains.'

'People like Joyce and Yeats and one or two others I could name, you mean? A hole?'

'They come in all shapes and sizes.'

'In the ground.'

'Where else?'

'This time of year, local soil, six feet long, three feet wide, three feet deep.'

'Yes . . . I can see that.'

'How long would it take to dig?'

'Depends.'

'On?'

'On the person, or persons, on the equipment . . . a weak person with a trowel would take a week, a man with a mechanical digger would take ten minutes.'

'Could it be dug in the hours of darkness at this time of year? Say six hours?'

'Possibly. A grave digger takes a full day to dig one grave.'

'Could you do it? The hole I described, I mean?'

'Possibly. But I didn't.'

'No?'

'No. Will that be all? I've got a business that's nose-diving.'

'Yes. For now.' Hennessey stood. 'I'd like to take a length of scaffolding from the rear of your vehicle.'

'So long as you bring it back.'

Hennessey drove to the Williamses' bungalow. He saw Yellich's fawn-coloured Escort, the other vehicles he didn't recognize. He saw the media being kept at bay by a blue and white police tape, all anxious to get footage and photographs and to see the Williamses' bungalow which was not unlike many thousands of similar bungalows in the United Kingdom. It was the interior of the building that mattered, yet here, for no reason that Hennessey could understand, was the media, anxious to see and to photograph a roof and a line of brickwork. He parked his car, pushed through the scrum of press and entered the house. Yellich stood in the hallway looking pleased with himself.

'Anything, Yellich?'

'Yes, boss. Something of great importance, something very solemn.'

'Oh?'

'It's a murder scene.' Toby Partridge peered at Hennessey from around a corner. At first a small, bespectacled head, as if disembodied from the rest of him, said, 'It's a murder scene,' and then he stepped round the corner from the bedroom into the hall and when, as if head and body were joined, he said, 'Oh yes, most definitely, it's a lovely, lovely murder scene.'

68

'Mr Partridge.' Hennessey raised his eyebrows at the short, slight figure of the man who he thought about twenty-four or -five.

'Doctor.' Partridge smiled. 'I've been doctored, oh yes. And this is as fine a murder scene as ever you'll find. Oh, yes.'

'You see what first put me onto it was the smell of bleach, even now you can discern it, but a few days ago it must have been overpowering.'

'It was,' Hennessey said. 'I thought it was a clean household.'

'Oh, it's more than that, oh yes.' Partridge danced about excitedly. 'I mean, what householders use bleach in this quantity? Few, I'll be bound. The point is that here something has been cleaned up. This house is a sanitized crime scene, oh yes, very much so. Then it was ransacked, but before it was ransacked it was the scene of a dreadful crime. So we ask ourselves, what has been tidied up?'

'A murder. Don't tell me.'

'Oh, I should think so. More than one, really. Can't fully sanitize a crime scene, very difficult, oh yes, oh my, yes, very difficult.' Partridge twitched nervously, rodent-like.

'You've made your point.' Hennessey found Partridge's nervous, excitable eccentricity difficult to take. That he was due to retire in a few years' time and would thus avoid Partridge when he, Partridge, would be in his thirties and forties and presumably even more unbearable than he is found to be at present, was a thought which was a source of some great comfort to Hennessey.

'Little, little . . . little.'

'What?'

'Specks . . . little . . . little . . . little . . . but everywhere.' Partridge waved his arms about as if conducting an orchestra. 'Tiny . . . tiny . . . specks.'

'Of?'

'Oh, blood. Oh yes . . . lots of them. The bleach has clearly cleaned up most of the mess, but blood has a habit of getting into the smallest of cracks, the most minute hole will be a home for a spot of blood. Found a lot under the carpet.'

'A lot?'

'Microscopically speaking. Under the edge of the carpet. A little in the cracks between the skirting board and the floor. There are two main areas of blood. Here in the hallway where we stand, at the entrance to the main bedroom. A lot of blood . . . microscopically speaking, we found around here . . . in all directions . . . the other main area is in the living room, just through here.' Partridge pushed between Yellich and Hennessey, a small figure between two towering police officers, and stood in the centre of the living room. 'Goes up as well as down,' he beamed.

'What does?'

'Blood. See.' He pointed to the ceiling. 'The person who cleaned this area of the home looked down, and all around, but didn't look up. There.'

'I don't see anything.' Hennessey looked at the ceiling.

'Well, there isn't anything to see.'

'Dr Partridge . . .' Hennessey growled.

'With the naked eye.'

'But with the aid of a lens held at close quarters, small specks of blood have been located.' He smiled an aren't-I-clever, smile. 'Taken samples, of course, sent them off to the forensic science laboratory at Wetherby. Of course.'

'Of course.'

'Went off by courier just before you arrived, boss,' Yellich explained. 'We've also got a latent.'

Hennessey smiled.

'It could belong to one the Williamses, but it's worth checking. Plenty of evidence that the person or persons who ransacked the house wore gloves, but there's a very recent-looking latent in the bathroom.'

'Very recent,' Partridge said. 'Noticeably more recent than any other latent and also different. The latent in question is a "loop", being one of the four classifications of fingerprints: "loops", "whirls", "arches" and "tented arches".'

'I know that.'

'Well, all the other prints in the house are "whirls", as if the Williamses, as a family, all had "whirls" as their fingerprint type, but the recent latent was made by someone with prints of the "loop" category. I pointed it out to your Scene of Crime Officer, he's lifting it now.'

'It's a promising point, boss,' Yellich said defensively of Dr Partridge. 'We have a house full of fingerprints of the "Whirl" type, a lot of prints made with gloved hands, and then one, just one, "loop" print in the bathroom.'

'If it was our man, who'd want to search a bathroom? What could be hidden in a bathroom?'

'Either he was being thorough, or he didn't search it. He took advantage of the facilities while he was in the house. It's been known before, burglars having loose bowels during a burglary, induced by the fear and tension of the act.'

'I'm aware of that, sometimes they even use the toilet.'

'I've known felons do more stupid things than take their gloves off for a second or two.'

'Yes . . .' Hennessey sighed. 'Indeed. So what was being searched for?'

'These.' Yellich held up a cellophane sachet containing photographs.

'I thought you looked pleased with yourself, Yellich.'

'Found them in the garden shed, sir.'

Hennessey took the photographs out of the sachet and held them carefully at the edges, making sure he prevented his own fingerprints getting on the surface or the reverse of the prints. 'Had a pleasant time together, didn't they?'

'Aye . . .' Yellich said. 'I recognize the bungalow in some of the photos, but the other location . . . it's like a studio . . . hardly any furniture . . . just a mattress on the floor.'

'It's the house Richardson built for Max Williams – I'll tell you the story. But it's clear from this that Mrs Williams and Tim Sheringham used it as a love nest.'

'Shall we pick Sheringham up, boss?'

'Not yet. Let's process that latent, if he's got track and if the latent is his, then we'll fondle his collar. Time for cautious treading, Yellich.'

'Anything you say, boss. How did you get on with Richardson?'

'Well, he's got a motive. Williams looks like he's destroyed his business.'

'Motive enough. I've known people murder for less.'

'So have I. He didn't say anything to implicate himself, but he didn't say anything to enable us to strike him off the list of suspects. He's still in the frame, as is Mr Sheringham. But mainly Sheringham.'

'Does he have an alibi for the time window?'

'Not for Sunday or the Monday or Tuesday evenings. His wife, very conveniently, was in Ireland. She arrived back this morning.'

'How convenient.'

'Isn't it? Give me an alibi merchant every time. If we can break the alibi we've won. No alibi means the heavy burden of proof rests on our shoulders. But he's a volatile man and he's got a lovely motive.'

'Love that word,' said Partridge. 'Lovely. It's a lovely word.'

Hennessey and Yellich glanced at each other. They had forgotten Partridge's presence.

That evening at home, Yellich was kneeling near an alcove in his house putting up shelves, as had long been requested by his wife, when his son approached him.

'Hiya, Jeremy,' Yellich smiled.

Jeremy beamed at his father.

Yellich held up a nail. 'Nail,' he said. 'Nail.'

'Nail,' repeated Jeremy. Yellich held up a hammer. 'Hammer.'

'Hammer.'

'Good boy.'

Jeremy Yellich walked away, looking pleased with himself. A few moments later he returned to where his father was working and picked up the hammer and said, 'Hammer.'

'Good lad.' Yellich put his arm round his son and kissed his forehead. 'Good, good boy.'

The younger man toyed with Oscar's ears as the dog allowed his head to rest on the man's lap. Hennessey put the coffee pot, and tray of milk and sugar and cups, down on the kitchen table.

'Names?' said the younger man, looking over the list of names that Hennessey had written.

'Something I thought I'd do out of interest. You see, I went through school from the age of eleven to sixteen with the same form, some left, one or two came, but to all intents and purposes, the thirty-two that finished were the same thirty-two that started. Each morning of every school day the register was taken, each morning the same thirty-two surnames were read out. I thought I'd try and remember them. As you see, I've recalled all but five or six.'

'You're getting old, Dad. You're looking back.'

'No, I'm not, I'm convincing myself my memory is still intact. He poured the coffee. So you're in Leeds tomorrow?'

'Yes, I'm going NG to the case you'll have read about, bloke set fire to his council house to force the council to give him another tenancy. Killed his two infant children in the process.'

'Yes, I read it.'

'The bloke says he's a victim of local hostility, and vigilantes tried to burn him out. The Crown case against him is overwhelming, but he belongs to that mind-set which, from childhood, believes that if you deny something you'll get away with it. It's far better to play with a straight bat and make a clean breast of things. As it is, he'll get two life sentences. He's told his solicitor to enter a NG plea, so his solicitor has instructed me and I dutifully take instructions and will have to challenge the Crown's case, which is not challengeable. But that's how our criminal justice system works.'

Hennessey sat down. 'What would happen if a felon were to say to a barrister, "Look I did it, but they can't prove it, so I want to plead not guilty."'

'Show him the door. If you went along with that you'd be misleading the court, wilfully so. You'd be finished as a silk.'

'I thought that. It's a pleasant evening, shall we have coffee on the lawn?'

Sitting on the wooden garden furniture chairs, the younger man said, 'You should have got married again, Dad.'

'Nothing could replace . . .' Hennessey smiled. 'I mean, *no one* could replace Jennifer.'

'But it couldn't have been easy for you, bringing me up alone.'

'It wasn't, and I loved every minute of it. And I had help; Mrs Last used to help a lot, I couldn't have done it without her.'

'I remember her. I was quite saddened by her death.'

'Well, you and she bonded with each other. It would have been quite a loss for you. But that's it, I'm not a needy person. I can live without a partner more easily than I can live with the wrong partner. And like I said . . . if I couldn't have Jennifer . . . we were very much in love, you know, your mother and I.'

'I know you were, Dad.'

'She planned the garden, you know.'

'You never told me that.'

'She did. When we moved into this house, the entire garden, the back garden, was just a greensward, a swathe of grass, could play a game of cricket on it. That's why I won't leave this house, not just because her ashes are scattered here, but because this garden is her design.'

'Well . . .' The young man watched a swallow loop and swoop.

'She was heavily pregnant, couldn't do anything except sit and read, and one day at the kitchen table she designed the garden. Reduced the lawn to half its original size, planting a privet from left to right with a gateway set in it, a potting shed and an orchard beyond the privet, and a waste area with a pond in the very bottom. The first apple trees were planted to coincide with your arrival, at least Jenn saw that. She used to walk with you amongst the saplings. Took me fully five years to complete it to her design.'

'The trees are as old as me then? Thirty years.'

'The oldest ones are, apple tree saplings are quite expensive and so we . . . I had to plant the orchard over time.'

'Still, you ought to have found someone.'

'Oh, I have.' Hennessey smiled at his son. He relished his company.

'Well, all the secrets are being exposed this evening. This *is* news.'

'It's a recent development. Still new.'

'Tell me about her.'

'She's a professional woman, divorced, three children who are old enough to know that their mum needs a partner and are not possessive of her. They've welcomed me into their family. I help out with the homework, and the like. Love it. She has three children, a high-powered, demanding job, a horse and two rabbits, so we've worked out that I come eighth on her list of priorities.'

Charles Hennessey smiled. 'You haven't lost your dry sense of humour, Dad. I think that has carried you through.'

'Probably has.' Hennessey glanced up at the crimson sky.

'Magnificent sunset.'

'Isn't it.'

'Tell me about Mum.'

'What can I say . . . a lovely, lovely woman . . . all she could do was give of herself, nurture things, husband, son, a garden, house plants . . . she just gave and gave and gave, and all she seemed to want in return was to see that the things she gave to thrived. That was all the reward she wanted.'

5

Thursday morning

... in which a suspect is quizzed and a double life is exposed.

The twin spools in the cassette tape recorder spun slowly, silently. The red light glowed.

'The date is Thursday, the eleventh of June, the time is ten-fifteen and the place is Micklegate Bar Police Station in the City of York. I am Chief Inspector Hennessey. I am going to ask the other people in the room to identify themselves.'

'Detective Sergeant Yellich.'

'Nathan Samual of Samual, Samual & Kileen, solicitors.'

'Tim Sheringham.' Said in a resentful, surly manner.

'Mr Sheringham, you have been arrested in connection with the murder of Mr and Mrs Williams.'

'So I understand.'

'Did you murder Mr and Mrs Williams?'

'No.'

Hennessey looked at Sheringham, such sudden long shots had paid off before. 'Thought you'd say that.

'Did you know Mr and Mrs Williams?'

'No.' Sheringham smiled. 'I didn't know them.' He emphasized the word 'them'.

'Did you know Mr Williams?'

'No.'

'Did you know Mrs Williams?'

'Yes. Very well indeed.'

'What do you mean?'

76

'I mean sexually. I knew her sexually. We had an affair. She enrolled at the gym. Things went from there.'

'I see. How long did you know Mrs Williams?'

'About two years, maybe longer. I didn't keep a diary.'

'When did the relationship finish?'

'Last week.'

'Why did it finish?'

'Because my wife was getting suspicious.'

'How did Mrs Williams react?'

'As you'd expect.'

'Mr Sheringham, I've been a police officer for many years, pretty well all my working life, and I have learned not to expect anything. So, how did she react?'

'Badly. She threw a tantrum. Screaming about the place.'

'The place?'

'Her little house.'

'The house or the bungalow?'

A pause. Then Tim Sheringham said, 'The house.'

'Did she threaten to tell your wife?'

'Probably. She was angry. I didn't really listen. She was angry because she'd spent a lot of money on me. I was her "boy". She bought me gifts and meals in upmarket restaurants. I showed her a good time. I gave her a good time. She gave me money and things.'

'She gave you money?'

'Yes. She bought my body. Why not? Men do it all the time. And anyway, wouldn't you want my body if you were a fifty-something woman with a drunkard for a husband?'

Hennessey didn't reply.

Sheringham smirked. 'I suppose you wouldn't really understand that, not being married and all, I mean, would you, Chief Inspector? You know the first time we did "it", it was at the bungalow. He came home earlier than expected, in a taxi, entered the house and curled up on the sofa, drunk as a lord. We just carried on and then went for a meal. He wasn't aware of anything going on at all. She told me that had been the first time she'd done "it" for many years, she said she had a lot of catching up to do.'

'And you helped her catch up?'

'Well . . . yes. Is there anything wrong with that? Look, I am not a Christian but that doesn't mean I'm a bad guy. She had money, she could afford it.'

Hennessey said nothing, but the word 'credit' crept into his mind. 'You didn't always spend time with her at the bungalow?'

'No. We met at a house her husband had had built. They had money. I told you. We started to use the house as soon as it was complete because she thought her neighbours were getting suspicious.'

'And she didn't take it too kindly when you broke it off?'

'Like I said, very unkindly. I mean, I was her possession, she'd take me to restaurants not just to buy me a meal, but to show me off. She used to enjoy the envious looks she'd get from other women.'

'I can imagine.'

'We went away once . . . a weekend . . . a hotel near the coast. Not actually on the coast itself, that was too near bed and breakfast land for her . . . but just inland, a mile or two inland from Scarborough. She paid.'

'She would by the sound of it.'

'Well, she'd have to, the gym is paying its way but only just and anyway, my wife and I have a joint account, I couldn't hide spending money on Amanda. I'm in trouble as it is. I don't know how I'm going to explain this.'

'How did you explain the weekend away to your wife?'

'Said it was a business trip. Anyway, we were not married then. I enjoyed it, we were both something on the side for each other, that was part of the fun . . . but she was getting too indiscreet . . . showing me off too much . . . I felt it was getting dangerous . . . coming to the gym very frequently. Daily almost, so I blew her out.'

'Then what did you do?'

'Got on with living my life. Running the gym.'

'So why did you go back to the bungalow after she and her husband had been murdered?'

78

Sheringham glanced at Nathan Samual, who said, 'Can you explain that question, Chief Inspector?'

'I'd be happy to. Your affair, Mr and Mrs Williams were murdered, their home was ransacked. We know that the house was sanitized after the murder, but we got a fingerprint from the bathroom.' Sheringham caught his breath.

'Remembering something, Mr Sheringham?'

'I'm not saying anything.'

'You see,' Hennessey continued. 'You see, not only was the house sanitized after the murder, it was kept in a fastidiously clean manner. Cleaned daily, I should think, especially the bathroom. And your client freely admits that latterly he was rendezvousing with Mrs Williams at a newly built house, not at the bungalow, so his fingerprints could not be in the bungalow by lawful means.'

'Accepted,' Nathan Samual said. He was a small, thin-faced man, dwarfed, it seemed to Hennessey, by the powerfully built Tim Sheringham whose T-shirt stretched over a muscular chest and revealed muscular arms.

'The print in the bathroom, that belonged to Mr Sheringham. It puts you in the house after the murder of the woman with whom you had just broken off your relationship.'

'No comment.'

'Why did you ransack the house?'

'No comment.'

'What were you searching for?'

'No comment.'

'You didn't take anything. Stopped burglarizing homes, have you?'

'No comment.'

'So what were you looking for?'

'No comment.'

Hennessey opened the file which lay on the table in front of him and took out a photograph and placed it on the table in front of Sheringham. Sheringham's jaw dropped, his eyes widened.

'There are quite a few like that. Clearly taken over quite a long time period, at the bungalow, at the house . . . some out of doors. Only you and Amanda Williams . . . never a third person, so the photographs were taken with a time-delayed shutter.'

'Yes . . . they were. She insisted. I knew it was a bad idea. She sent them away to be developed, there's a company in London that will print anything. Pretty well, they draw the line at children.'

'I'm relieved to hear it.'

'Is this what you were looking for? This and the others? We found them in the garden shed, by the way.'

Sheringham gasped.

'They were not in the house at all. So what was it? Black-mail?'

Sheringham nodded.

'Could you speak for the benefit of the tape?'

'Yes.'

'How much did she want in return for the photographs?'

'Nothing. She didn't need money.'

'What then?'

'Me. She wanted me to agree to continue our affair, just carrying on as we had been doing, every Wednesday. You can understand it. How could a woman like that replace a man like me? She was going to send them to my wife. Look, I'm thirsty . . . how about . . .'

Hennessey reached for the off button and said, 'The time is eleven-oh-five a.m. The interview is being suspended for refreshments to be taken.' He switched off the tape recorder.

Sheringham and Nathan Samual remained in the interview room, sipping coffee out of white plastic beakers. Hennessey and Yellich stood in the corridor.

'What do you think, boss?' Yellich held his beaker of coffee in both hands.

'He's definitely in the frame for it, very definitely. He had something to fear from Mrs Williams. He's arrogant enough to murder, he's strong enough to dig the grave . . . he battered her over the head and he felled Mr Williams because he was there. He's got more of a motivation than Richardson because with Richardson things couldn't get worse. With Sheringham things could get an awful lot worse . . . Richardson isn't out of the frame but if you ask me, Sheringham's a stronger candidate. Fear, you see, Yellich, fear feeds the imagination, that leads to desperation and desperate men do desperate things. I can see him doing it. He's full of himself, has a lot to lose, pops 'em both off as the only safe thing to do. Sanitizes the house, then collects the bodies a day or two later, drives them out to a field and buries them. Then he returns looking for the photographs of himself and her in happier times and, during the search, leaves a careless but very convenient fingerprint in the bathroom.'

Then Yellich said quietly, 'Do you think they might be in it together, boss?'

Hennessey's eyes narrowed. 'Tell me more, Yellich.'

'Well, I once came across an Arabic proverb: the enemy of my enemy is my friend.'

'Go on.' Hennessey sipped his coffee.

'They're both members of the business community in York. If they're known to each other, they both have motivation to murder the Williamses . . . they're both strong enough to dig the grave, but sharing the job would make it a cakewalk. Together, they'd make light of it. It's also a big crime scene to sanitize, two guys would be better employed at it than one. Just thinking aloud, boss.'

Hennessey beamed at him. 'Yellich, on occasions you please me greatly.'

'I do, boss?'

'Yes, Yellich. You do. Two heads are always better than one. Maybe for Richardson and Sheringham, as well as for you and me. I'll continue here.'

'Yes, boss.'

'You go and have a chat with Mrs Sheringham at the gym. Tease out what you can, but be discreet.'

'Yes, boss.'

'York is a small city; you're right, they may very well be known to each other, a link between them will be interesting. Very interesting indeed.'

Hennessey dropped his plastic mug into the waste bin beside the hot beverage vending machine and returned to the interview room. He switched the recording machine on as he sat down, the spools turned, the red light glowed. 'The interview recommences at eleven-twenty a.m. in the absence of Detective Sergeant Yellich. I am Chief Inspector Hennessey. I am now going to ask the other people in the room to identify themselves.'

'Nathan Samual.'

'You know who I am,' Sheringham growled.

'Just state your name for the tape, please.'

'Tim Sheringham. Happy now, old man?'

'Thank you. So, Mr Sheringham, you don't deny that Mrs Williams was a source of trouble for you?'

'I don't deny it.'

'So you have benefited from her death?'

'I've benefited from those photographs not being sent to my wife.'

'But she did threaten to speak to your wife.'

'No comment.'

'It's not unreasonable of me to assume that she did make such a threat.'

'Assume what you like.'

'So it's not therefore unreasonable of me to assume that you have benefited from her death. She can't talk to your wife from beyond the grave.'

'She can't.'

'So a weight is off your mind?'

'Yes . . . yes . . . if you like. But not fully, you know it's possible that Vanessa will find out . . . your past has a way of catching up with you.'

'As you well know.' Hennessey took a sheet of paper from the file. 'Your previous convictions.'

'A lot of them are spent.'

'A lot are . . . but there's quite a pattern of violence, isn't there? And burglary. Aggravated burglary. And you are, are you not, just the sort of person who'd batter the life out of someone and then ransack their house?'

82

'I object to that question.' Nathan Samual spoke softly, yet with no small measure of authority.

'I've calmed down,' Sheringham said coldly. 'The gym's seen to that. And marriage. My last spell inside I spent as much time as I could pushing weights, working on my body culture. A guy in there said I could earn big money if I could open a gym. I'm not making as much as he reckoned I would, but enough. I'm making more straight pennies than I ever made bent pennies.'

'I'm gratified to hear it . . . but the potential's there. Now, tell me about this offence, which is not spent. The conviction a few years ago for the misuse of a controlled substance.'

'A few ounces of cannabis, for my own consumption, I hasten to add. I wasn't selling it.'

'Still known to Mr McCarty though.'

'Of the Drug Squad?'

'The one and the same.'

'I've had the pleasure once or twice.'

'But nothing current?'

'Of course.'

'Of course.' Hennessey smiled. 'But let's return to your potential.'

'Potential?'

'For violence . . . that's been your history. You have not hesitated to attack someone if they annoyed you.'

'I've calmed down.'

'To batter someone to death because they threatened to ruin you?'

'Wouldn't you?'

'So you did!'

'No, I didn't.'

'"Wouldn't you", implies you did.'

'It implies nothing,' Nathan Samual said solemnly.

'Even so,' Hennessey pressed forward, 'we have assault, grievous bodily harm, malicious damage . . . not the sort of person you'd want to meet in one of the snickelways on a dark night, are you?'

'I can look after myself.'

'Or on a dance-hall floor.'

'I don't dance.'

'Or inside your home.'

'I didn't kill them.'

'Where were you on Sunday afternoon?'

'I went for a run by the river.'

'Anybody see you?'

'Plenty.'

'Anybody that recognized you, that could offer an alibi? What about your wife?'

'At the gym. Wednesdays and Sundays are ladies' days, both are long days for her.'

'Other days it's mixed?'

'Yes. The customers like it that way. A lot of relationships have started in the gym.'

'I can imagine. Yourself and Amanda Williams being an example of same.'

'You should come down, free session, I'll take you round the circuit, maybe you'll want to enrol. You'll be the oldest there, but you never know your luck, some women go for the older man, they want a father figure.'

'As some men go for the older woman, eh, Mr Sheringham?'

'Only if they have dosh.' Smiling, provoking, game playing. 'What about it, fancy a trip round the circuit?'

'No, I don't.'

'Well, don't say I didn't make the offer. It's no good at the end of your life saying, "I wonder what would have happened if . . ."'

'Full of wisdom for one so young, aren't you?'

'I was born old, like Merlin the Magician. I get younger by the day.'

'Where were you on Monday and Tuesday night?'

'At home.'

'Alone?'

'With my wife.'

'She'll vouch for that?'

'She may.'

'May?'

'She's a heavy sleeper. She'll sleep through an earthquake. Me, I suffer from insomnia from time to time. Not every night, but some nights. There's been times when I've been unable to sleep, I've got up, gone out for a six-mile run, come back, showered, got back into bed, grabbed a couple of hours' sleep and we've woken up together and she hasn't realized I've been away.'

'So you may not have an alibi for Monday and Tuesday night either?'

'No. But I don't need one. I didn't kill anybody, see?'

'No. Actually, I don't see.

'Can you drive a car?'

'I have the ability, but no licence.'

'Disqualified, part of the malicious damage incident, it says here.'

'Guy cut me up at the lights. So I sorted his car. Thought I'd be less likely to get a prison sentence if I only damaged his metal, rather than him.'

'Seemed to work. Heavy fine but you avoided the slammer. You have access to your car?'

'Yes.'

'So it's not impossible for you to have gone to the Williamses' bungalow to silence Amanda Williams who was threatening to expose your affair and silence her in the best way you could think of, and then to silence Max Williams because he was unfortunate enough to be there. And it's not impossible for you to have slipped out of your house on Monday night to sanitize the crime scene, because there'd have been blood everywhere, and it's not impossible to have slipped out of the house on Tuesday to bury the bodies.'

'No.' Sheringham smiled. 'It's not impossible but you'll never prove it.'

'Why, did you cover your tracks well enough?'

'Because I didn't do it.'

'Double murder. Rotten thing to have on your conscience.'

'I wouldn't know.'

'Did you have eye contact just before you killed them?'

'Don't answer that.' Nathan Samual turned to Sheringham.

Then to Hennessey he said, 'That's a leading question, Chief Inspector.'

'Which one was first, Sheringham?'

'Really, Chief Inspector, I protest at this line of questioning.' Samual turned to Hennessey and, somewhat imperiously, Hennessey thought, said, 'Chief Inspector, I really have to insist that at this point you must decide whether to charge my client or terminate this interview until you have more evidence.'

'There is a fingerprint in the bathroom.' Hennessey leaned back in his chair. 'That is evidence of unlawful entry.'

'Not when my client has been a regular visitor to the house.'

Hennessey reached for the off switch of the tape recorder. 'This interview is terminated at eleven-forty a.m.' He switched off the machine, the spools stopped turning, the red light faded. 'Very well, your client is free to leave the police station. But this is not the end of the matter, please understand that.'

Liam McCarty was a well-set man in his forties, short hair, grey suit. He was a sergeant in the City of York Police Drug Squad. He and Hennessey knew each other just well enough to be on first-name terms. Hennessey tapped on the door of McCarty's office and sat in the chair in front of McCarty's desk.

'Come in and sit down,' said McCarty with a smile.

Hennessey returned the smile. 'Tim Sheringham?' he said.

'Sheringham . . . Sheringham . . . bells ring, George, but I can't place him.'

'Sheringham's Gym. He's a suspect in a code four one. We put his details into the computer and, among other things, he came up as an alert to you and the good men and women of the DS.'

'Yes . . . that Sheringham.' McCarty stood and walked to a filing cabinet, opened it, and extracted a file and handed it to Hennessey.

'Well, well . . .' Hennessey looked at the grainy black and

white photographs in the file which showed Tim Sheringham and Max Williams talking to each other, on a park bench, inside a café, walking in the centre of York, walking the walls. 'So they knew each other? He's in much more deeply than he's letting on. What's the story here?'

'Incomplete as yet, but we believe that Williams was funding an anabolic steroids racket, and I mean big time, putting up money for large-scale purchase of the stuff which Sheringham was then knocking out to the gym customers. We have a couple of guys in the gym, posing as members. Not enough evidence for an arrest yet, but we were focusing on Williams, we had him in for a quiz session . . . he's easy meat, no bottle at all . . . we just let him know that he was under suspicion . . . just to put the pressure on him, a slight turn of the screw . . . we floated the possibility of immunity from prosecution in return for information and a statement implicating Sheringham. He's a rising drug baron in the Famous and Faire and we're looking to nip him before he rises much further.'

'Talk about the left hand not knowing what the right hand is doing.'

'Well, you do know, we registered our interest, had it entered on the computer which is why he came up as an alert to us. Why, what's happened?'

'Just that the guy we believe Sheringham has filled in is none other than Max Williams.'

'Well, there's your motivation. If he thought Williams was going to blow the whistle on him, and Sheringham's a nasty piece of work, he wouldn't hesitate to off someone if he thought it would save him from a stretch as a guest of Her Majesty.'

'It's a far stronger motivation than we thought. Makes more sense – he was into Williams's wife . . . playing away from home . . . he walked out on her and we believe Amanda Williams threatened to tell Mrs Sheringham of the affair she had had with her husband. We believe he killed her to stop that and her husband just got in the way somehow. Now it appears that he had a motivation to ice them both.'

'Vanessa Sheringham's a formidable woman. Have you met her?' McCarty sat back in his chair. 'She has some control over him, can't work it out, but she's the major-domo in the relationship.'

'My sergeant's interviewing her right now. But you know this could well clinch the case against Sheringham, he had a motive to murder them both. She was going to inform on him to his wife and he was going to inform on him to the police. What better solution than to batter the life out of the both of them?'

'What better? Is he in custody?'

'No. Don't want to bring him in too early, don't want to start the clock ticking until I'm on sure footing.'

'And he's not going anywhere . . . I can understand your caution.'

'Have him in for another chat, though. We'll be doing that in the light of this. What have you got on Sheringham from your perspective?'

'Not enough. We believe that anabolic steriods have been seeping out of Sheringham's Gym for a while now. Then one of our informers, he told us that a larger than normal amount had been shifted and the money bags was a guy called Williams. He has, or I should say, had, a reputation in the Vale for being something of a good touch for finance.'

'He had.'

'Anyway, all that consignment had been moved when we heard that Sheringham was twisting Williams's arm, wanting him to fund a much larger shipment. Usual deal, Williams got his investment back plus twenty per cent once the stuff had been sold, but Williams may well be a good touch but he's scared of the law. I got the impression that he was desperate to recover some money and was flirting with crime as a consequence, silly man. Anyway, we had him in here, a little off-the-record chat, offered him a deal, asked him to fund Sheringham, we'll keep Sheringham under close surveillance, and when he makes the purchase we'll pounce: we'll get Sheringham and his supplier and the steroids, Williams gets his money back plus immunity from prosecution.'

'Not a bad deal.'

'That's what we thought. He said he'd think it over. That was just last week sometime.'

Hennessey stood. 'Well, thanks, Liam. Owe you one. Time for a second chat with Sheringham.'

Yellich found Vanessa Sheringham a very attractive woman. She would, he thought, be attractive in any man's eyes. He thought her perhaps five foot eight or nine inches tall, angular features, high cheekbones, a mane of dark, glowing hair, blue eyes. She sat in the office of Sheringham's Gym wearing a blue leotard with silver tights and a pair of blue and white trainers that didn't look as though they were ever worn out of doors. She wore an expensive-looking wristwatch and equally expensive-looking engagement and wedding rings. The watch and the rings were balanced by gold bracelets on the right wrist. By her smile, by the gleam in her eyes, Yellich knew that she was enjoying his eyes upon her. The woman knew she was beautiful. He disliked her intensely. It was Yellich's experience that great beauty goes hand in hand with great cruelty and great selfishness. It had been his emotionally scarring experience to have once had an involvement with a photogenically beautiful woman, an actress, he remembered, and he had found her, and recalled her, as being self-obsessed and volatile, usually in public; making a meal out of issues other people would make light of. Yellich, looking back, if not at the time, saw her as a woman who would never know contentment, and would only approach happiness if she was on a pedestal, enjoying universal attention and approval, and getting her own way. She had been, in fact, the ugliest person to have crossed his life's path. It had been a salutary lesson and while, since then, he had continued to enjoy the images of human female perfection, he did not yearn for any form of contact, physical or emotional, with a woman of this kind. And here in front of him was one such, enjoying his attention, and the annoying thing about it for Yellich was that she believed he was thinking exactly the opposite of what he was actually thinking.

'So, you've arrested my husband?' She smiled, but haughtily so.

'Not yet. He is helping with enquiries.'

'He once told me what that phrase meant. The first time he helped the police with their enquiries, he was fifteen and a policeman threatened to break his arm unless he confessed to a crime he hadn't committed.'

'No comment,' Yellich said coldly. 'So you help your husband in the gym?'

'No.'

'No?' Yellich glanced to his left through the pane of glass at men and women in brightly coloured sportswear pushing weights and running on small conveyor belts, moving to music with a strong beat.

'No. He helps *me* run the gym. It's my gym. We are married but the gym is mine. It belongs to me, lock, stock and barrel. I'm a wealthy woman, I was when I married him. He was not a wealthy man, he comes from Tang Hall, he's still there in his mind. My father's a businessman, farming equipment, has a house in Nether Poppleton.'

'Different side of the tracks. Literally.'

'Yes. He's lucky to have me, don't you think? I am a woman with everything, looks, charm, money. He's a nice hunk of man flesh . . . he at least looks the part.'

'Appearance means a lot to you, does it?'

'It means everything. Appearance and money. But I'm secure. If I divorce him and cast him out into the great unknown, he goes back to Tang Hall and crime. And he knows it. I can control him. If he steps out of line he's by himself. He dare not even look at another woman. Are you married?'

'Yes.'

'Is your wife pretty?'

'No.'

Vanessa Sheringham smiled.

'She's beautiful. She's a very beautiful woman. In every way.'

'I see, the old "eye of the beholder" number . . .'

'We'll keep this official if you don't mind, Mrs Sheringham.'

'As you wish.' Just then the music in the gym suddenly stopped.

'Your husband can't be very secure in his marriage. I mean, from what you're telling me, if you were to divorce he has no claim, even in part, on the house or the gym.'

'He doesn't. Both were my possession before we married and he has signed a contract that should we divorce he will not lay claim to either. He gave his name to the gym because it has a certain ring to it. Before that it was called "Vanessa's Gym", but Sheringham's is a little classier sounding. Don't you think?'

'Perhaps.' But privately he conceded that names of products are very, very important in terms of marketing strategy. That was why dog fish used to be sold as 'rock salmon'. When the practice was outlawed, nobody bought dog fish, though they'd been eating the inexpensive and highly nutritious 'rock salmon' for generations, so Yellich had once read.

'But yes, I suppose he is a little insecure.' Vanessa Sheringham turned to her side and replaced another compact disc in the hi-fi machine – once again, music of a strong beat and rhythm played loudly in the gym. 'But I like that, you know.' She smiled as she once again turned towards Yellich. 'It keeps him on his toes, he's very attentive. I'm happy with the arrangement. He's not, but that's the way I like it. I'm not prepared to surrender the least bit of control.'

'What I'm driving at is that your husband has a lot of motivation to keep you happy?'

'Yes.' Vanessa Sheringham nodded. 'That I like . . . a lot of motivation to keep me happy. He's nothing without me, and an awful lot of women would be queuing up to fill my shoes. Not only because of what nature has given me, but because I have a fit, healthy and a handsome husband who will do my least bidding because he's terrified of our marriage ending. That's power. Power is lovely, it's as profound as an orgasm.'

'That's very interesting.' Yellich spoke softly. 'Very interesting indeed.'

'Power is, I've always liked power.'

'No, I meant that your husband would do much to keep his marriage alive.'

'Oh, he would. He comes from poverty, he's frightened of going back to it. One step out of line, as I said, and he can kiss goodbye to the good life.'

'He must be totally faithful to you?'

'Like I said, Mr Yellich, my husband would not even dare to look at another woman.'

'Can you tell me how many members you have?'

'Two hundred. About.'

'As many as that?'

'They don't all come at once.'

'So I see.'

'Members book in for one-hour sessions. We can accommodate thirty at any one time, we're open from eight a.m. to ten at night. So you see, we can accommodate more than twice our membership in one working day, but with about two hundred members, the gym doesn't get crowded. They pay an annual subscription, plus an entrance fee each time they come. We also sell snacks and hot drinks and sportswear. We do all right. We . . . I have a nice, steady growth rate. My husband may give the impression that we're struggling, but that's Tang Hall man speaking. If you grow up in Tang Hall, you rapidly learn to keep quiet about your money, if you've got any.'

'Can I have a look at the membership list?'

'Do you have a warrant?'

'No. I can get one, then we'll search the gym, who knows what steroids we'll find?'

'You won't find any.' Vanessa Sheringham reached for a drawer in a filing cabinet. 'But you can have a look at the list. Male or female?'

'Male, for now.'

'That relieves me.'

'Oh?'

'Yes.' Vanessa Sheringham handed Yellich a sheet of paper containing a list of names and addresses. 'Well, if you've arrested my husband, or he's at least helping you with your enquiries, and you wanted a list of my female members, then I'd start to get a little worried that I might have to divorce him. I mean, who knows what he's been up to?'

'Who indeed?' Yellich scanned the list of names. 'Or what indeed?' He found the 'Rs'. Michael Richardson's name came between John Richards and Donald Rye. 'May I keep this?'

'Yes. We have other lists.'

'What does your husband do in his free time?'

'He doesn't have any free time. The only two days of the week when he's not here with me at the gym are Wednesdays and Sundays, they're our ladies-only days. On those days he's addressing a list of jobs I leave for him. I add on, he does and ticks off when done. In any order he likes, keeps him busy about the house or collecting things. That's how we work it, that's how I like it.'

Yellich stood and said he'd see himself out.

Louise D'Acre took the length of scaffolding and held it against the linear fracture on the top of Amanda Williams's skull. She rotated it along its length over the skull. 'It's a little wide,' she said. She wore a green smock, the laboratory smelled of formaldehyde. Behind her, the laboratory assistant, Mr Filey, dutifully arranged surgical instruments on a trolley. 'It's possible,' she added. 'It's not impossible but I cannot say that it was this or any other length of scaffolding which killed her. I've a better chance of identifying the murder weapon by examining her skull than his, the single blow, you see, classic case of going out like a light, left a neat injury. His head was battered repeatedly. His death might have been prolonged.'

'Prolonged?' Hennessey asked.

'By a few seconds, but a second is a long time, long enough to know what's happening to you and if you're conscious for four or five seconds, then it's long enough to feel emotion.'

'Such as fear?'

'Such as terror, such as the certainty of death this instant . . . knowing you haven't the time to prepare for it. He knew what was happening to him. She, on the other hand, either

93

did or did not know what happened to her husband. His head was battered out of shape . . . there was real passion there. In fact, his skull reminded me of the Choctaw Indian skulls. They were apparently one of the east coast tribes of what is now the USA. One of the early victims of the Pilgrim Fathers either by way of execution or the measles. But they used to flatten their skulls with tight bindings, in much the same way that the Chinese used to bind the feet of their girl children. Max Williams's skull reminded me of the Choctaw Indian skull I once saw in a museum of anthropology. It was battered out of shape, which may or may not have been instantaneous. But she, bless her, was despatched by means of a single blow. Probably with something thinner than a length of scaffolding.'

She handed the piece of metal back to Hennessey.

'Thanks, Dr D'Acre.' Hennessey slipped the scaffolding pipe back into the holdall he had used to carry it from his car into the hospital, to the department of pathology.

'Why pick on a length of scaffolding as the murder weapon?'

'Oh, just that one of our suspects was seen and heard threatening Mr Williams with just such an object.'

'Fair enough, but the murder weapon, if you find it, will be covered with blood and hair and possibly slivers of bone from Mrs Williams. I was able to obtain some grit and oil from the back of the heads of both the Williamses.'

'Really?'

'Yes. Would have faxed you, still will, but I did note that they were laid face up on a cold surface soon after death, that accounts for the hypostasis on the posterior aspects of both bodies. If there is a garage adjoining their home, then that's where they were laid.'

'There is.'

'Might be worth getting the Scene of Crime people to give it the once-over.'

'Might well.'

'So you've got a suspect already?'

'Got two, in fact. Both have motives and Sergeant Yellich has had the inspired notion that if we can link the two together, then we can really build a case, at least we can begin to. The only problem is that they're not going to cough and neither of them are alibi merchants. They know the value of leaving the burden of proof with the police.'

'Hard life you have. If my customers don't tell me what I need to know, I can always put them back on ice, and pick my colleagues' brains, or just leave them until medical science advances and tells us . . . oh . . . I'm sorry . . .'

'No problem.' Hennessey smiled. 'Don't worry about it.'

6

Thursday afternoon

. . . in which Sergeant Yellich feels he travels back in time and Chief Inspector Hennessey meets a pleasantly unpleasant individual.

'A bit like Humpty Dumpty before the fall.' Yellich swilled his coffee around in his mug. 'Milady's view of the world is a little askew, as is her view of her place in it.'

'Sounds like it.'

'When her eyes are opened, she'll have a great fall and she just won't get put together again no matter how many horses and men His Highness can offer.'

'But there's a link between Richardson and Sheringham. Your intuition is paying off, Sergeant. It's paying off handsomely. Handsomely.' Hennessey leaned forwards on his desk and beamed at Yellich. 'We're still a tad short of evidence though. I couldn't hold Sheringham.'

'Not even with the fingerprint in the bathroom?'

'Not if he had been a regular visitor to the house. His solicitor jumped on that point, pounced, fell on it like a sparrowhawk.'

'Fair enough, I suppose.'

'Annoying though. But onwards and upwards – we're getting there Yellich, we're getting there. And the motivation is strong now, very strong, especially for Sheringham: he was scared that Max Williams was going to blow the whistle on him to the Drug Squad and he was scared that Amanda

Williams was going to blow the whistle on him to his old lady. Makes him something of a Taipan in my mind.'

'A what, sir?'

'A Taipan, it's an Australian snake. It's just a nugget of information I stored away. You see, snake venom falls into two distinct categories, apparently. One that paralyses the nervous system, and one that coagulates the blood preventing it being pumped round the body.'

'Blimey.'

'As you say. The Taipan isn't the most venomous snake in the world in terms of the strength of its poison, but it's the only snake in the world whose venom is double acting. It both coagulates the blood of its victim, and paralyses the central nervous system and that makes it the most deadly snake in the world. Sheringham is like that, he's got a double motivation.'

'And Richardson too. He wasn't a million miles from suspicion in the Kerr case, as you've pointed out. A man who owed Richardson money is found in a field with his head smashed in and his brains sticking out. And now Williams owes Richardson money and his head is also smashed to a pulp. That's too much of a coincidence, Sergeant. And both would, in a sense, be more angry with Max Williams than Amanda.'

'That would tie in with what Dr D'Acre said. You know, Mr Williams was murdered passionately, Mrs Williams coldly. One single, neat blow to the head would enable Sheringham to sleep at night. But Richardson's anger would make him want to repeatedly batter Max Williams, and keep battering him, long after he's dead. Then they team up and tidy the house, sanitize the crime scene and dig the grave, easy job for men built like they're built. Pity they're not stupid enough to alibi each other.'

'We've still got to get the Crown Prosecution Service to run with it, it's not for nothing that the CPS is known as the Criminal Protection Society in the canteen and the Police Club.' Hennessey paused. 'You look worried, Yellich.'

'I am. It's the cleaning of the house, sir.'

'What about it?'

'Well, it's not actually politically correct.'

'Cleaning a house?'

'No . . . my point. It's not politically correct.'

'Come on, within these four walls, out with it.'

'Well, boss, it has a woman's touch to it.'

Hennessey paused. 'It does, doesn't it?'

'I just can't see the likes of Richardson or Sheringham being efficient with a cloth and a bottle of disinfectant.'

'I can't either.'

'Mrs Richardson!' Both men spoke at once and held eye contact as they did so.

Hennessey completed it for both of them. 'It was her livelihood that went down the tubes as well. By the sounds of it, Mrs Sheringham would be more likely to murder her husband than either of the Williamses, nor can I see her being handy with the housework, that sort always has a "woman who does". Is that the phrase?'

'Mrs Richardson claims she was in Ireland over the weekend. If that alibi can be broken we're on our way, boss.'

'We are indeed.'

'So what do we do now, boss, pick her up?'

'Yes.' Hennessey sat back in his chair. 'Or do we? I wonder? No. Look, you seem to have a way with the ladies . . .'

'I wouldn't say that, boss.' Yellich grinned.

'You did well with Mrs Sheringham, you got the measure of her, allright. Go and see Mrs Richardson, take the measure of her. Me, I'm going to Selby.'

'Selby?'

'Selby. "Shored-up" has contacted me. Reckons he's got information to sell. You know him and his games . . . but he's come up with the goods before. And the weather's fine, and Selby's a pleasant little town. It's certainly better than the last place we met. Have you ever been to Doncaster on a rainy day in January?'

'No, can't say I have, boss.'

'Don't. When you've seen her, visit his bank.'

*   *   *

Yellich had to keep reminding himself to keep an open mind. The phrase 'salt of the earth' kept occurring to him when he spoke to Mrs Richardson. Yet he was all too well aware that the most unlikely people had committed desperate, terrible crimes. In his early days as a fresh-faced constable, he had allowed first impressions to cloud his judgement and let possible suspects go on their way only to find later that they had committed the crime in question and had slithered out of the arms of the law with a display of relaxed innocence. Now, with some years' service behind him, did he accept that everybody can commit crime, and even the most unlikely person will do so. Reluctantly, he accepted the police-canteen culture which states that, "They're all guilty unless you know otherwise. And I mean *know*".'

'There's no point in denying it, son.' Colleen Richardson was a tall, well-built, large-boned woman, who sat in a leather armchair in the front room of her Georgian-style house at the entrance of a new build estate on the edge of Huntingdon. A Persian cat slunk into the room and hopped silently onto Yellich's lap.

'That means he likes you,' Mrs Richardson smiled. She spoke with a strong Irish accent. 'Not all our visitors get that treatment. I tend to let my animals do my thinking for me. I've found over the years that if they like someone then that person is allright, and they've never been proved wrong. Female intuition is nothing compared to animal instinct. But if she annoys you, lift her off.'

'She doesn't bother me.' Yellich stroked the cat's ears and back. The beast began to purr softly. He pondered that cats are nice creatures unless you happen to be a mouse. Your view depends on your standpoint. Mrs Richardson, with her pleasant manner and very well-appointed home, with framed black and white photographs of old Ireland – a man on a cycle, on an endless rural track, another which could be anywhere but was entitled 'Phoenix Park 1912' – may well be a nice woman, unless you were her victim. Then he said, 'No point in denying it. What do you mean?'

Colleen Richardson reached for a cigarette from a cigarette

box which was far too elaborately designed for Yellich's taste, and lit it with a cigarette lighter of the type which, he thought, had gone out of fashion many years earlier. A huge paperweight of a contraption, conventional mechanism at the top but a body as big as an orange, and the colour of same. 'No point in denying it. He hated Williams. I've never known two things about my husband. I've never known any reason to fear him, and I've never known him capable of hate. The Williamses came into our lives and I knew both. Reckon after twenty-something years of marriage, I finally knew my husband. But they say that you never really know the person you live with, either they keep changing so they're one step ahead of you, or you keep discovering something new about them. But Michael didn't kill them.'

'How do you know?'

'I know what I just said, but I do know my husband well enough to know that he didn't kill them. He's got a terrible temper, but if he was violent I would have seen *that* by now, surely to God. I mean, he's been in a few pub fights when he's been too much in the black stuff and when he was a youth, but nothing since and nothing when he's been sober.' She inhaled deeply and exhaled slowly. 'To think that when I went away to Ireland I thought things couldn't be worse. Michael's business in the bog, us having to sell this house to pay his crew and supplies, and this, the home we'd worked so hard for . . . Michael built these houses, did you know?'

'I didn't.'

'Two streets, for young or junior professional people, he picked out a corner plot for this house. Extra bit of land, you see . . . so I went to see my old father in Galway, told him things couldn't get worse and sure, when I came back he's become a murder suspect. Just shows, when you think you're on the bottom, when you think it can't get any worse, you get pushed down even further . . . I mean, in the name of the Holy Mother, where is the justice in that? Is there justice in the world, let me ask you that?'

'We haven't charged your husband with anything, Mrs Richardson.'

'Being a suspect is bad enough. Thank the Almighty our children are away so they don't see this.'

'Where are they?'

'Leeds. They're flapping their wings, their father taught them the trade, so they've moved away. Richardson Brothers, Builders, Leeds. Sure, I can see Michael asking them for a job. You'll be making a case against Michael?'

'No. That's old-fashioned police thinking.' Yellich continued to stroke the cat and then stopped and lifted the beast from his lap. It occurred to him that by favouring Mrs Richardson's pet he was blurring professional boundaries. The cat arched its back in indignation and curled up on the deep pile carpet in front of the hearth into which Yellich noted that Mrs Richardson was in the habit of throwing her cigarette butts. 'We used to do that. Identify a suspect, try to build a case against him, if we could we'd run with it. Now we tie.'

'Tie?'

'TIE. Trace. Interview. Eliminate. Cast a wide net, trace anybody and everybody who has some connection with the crime, interview them, and if we can't eliminate them we . . . look at them a little more closely.'

'And Michael?'

'He hasn't been eliminated.'

'So he's a suspect?'

'Yes.'

'In the name . . . he lost more fights than he won. Often he went down to men half his size. We're ruined. Finished. Now this . . .'

'So your husband's business is finished?'

'Aye. So he says. A couple of little jobs, but that won't pay the bills. So the house, our home, it'll have to be sold. We came with nothing, we'll go with nothing.'

'He could sell the house he built for Max Williams?'

'Not at a profit. And anyway, the house is just too fancy, a lot of fixtures and fittings, sunken baths and gold-plated taps. It'll not sell well in this part of England. In the south, maybe, but the north of England, those sort of knick-knacks just are not to folks' taste. He could sell it, to be sure, but

101

at such a loss . . . Michael thinks we'll be better off selling this house, but we want this house, not Williams's fairy-tale design. See, the upshot is that we're finished and that's down to Williams.'

'It's like your husband blundered into something.'

'That's putting it mildly.' Colleen Richardson took one last deep drag on the half-smoked nail and flicked the still burning butt into the fire grate where it smouldered harmlessly into extinction. 'See, Williams has a . . . had a reputation in the Vale for being a good touch.'

'A good touch?'

'For money.'

'Oh, yes?'

'Aye, so he was. A lot of businesses have been started up and kept going in the Vale over the last ten years or so using Williams's money as seed money. His name is well-known by businessmen in the Vale. See, that's why Michael went ahead and built the house, Williams's reputation, his money supply was endless. Williams must have known what he was doing, must have to make money like he could throw it around. It was like he was making the stuff . . . Michael said he bought into companies when they were new, helped them off the ground, rode piggyback and then sold his share, or his shares, when they were up and running with full order books. Reckon that's how Michael got in so deeply, based on Williams's reputation.'

'Reckon that's it. Tell me, did your husband ever mention a fella by the name of Sheringham?'

'The man at the gym? That's the only Sheringham we know.'

'What is your husband's relationship with him?'

'Tim Sheringham? Drinking partners. There's some age gap between them. Twenty years or so. More. They met at the gym. Tim's the owner, I think. They occasionally went for a beer after Michael had been for his workout. Michael always booked in for the last session, nine till ten, so there was an hour's troughing time left. That's how stupid men are. All that good done to their little bodies and then they go to the pub and undo it all. But Michael and Tim Sheringham were not in business or anything.'

'But they knew each other in a social manner?'

'Oh, yes.'

'Do you know when they last went out together?'

'Last week, last Thursday evening. That's Michael's night at the gym.'

'You were in York then?'

'Yes.'

'Not in Ireland?'

'No. Left for Ireland on the Friday. Returned yesterday.'

'Your father will vouch for that?'

'What's that supposed to mean?' Colleen Richardson flushed with anger.

'What I said. He'll vouch for that if we contact the Gardaí in Galway, ask them to call on him, he'll tell them that you were with him?'

'He'll tell them nothing. They'll need to get where he is before he'll speak to them.'

'Meaning?'

'Meaning he's in the ground, God rest him. He died a year ago this weekend gone and I was not there, God forgive me. I went to his graveside and I told him how I was, how I was not.'

'Who else did you speak to?'

'Nobody. I stayed in his wee terraced house. It still belongs to us while we contact two of my brothers to sort the estate.'

'So nobody can confirm you were in Ireland?'

'No. You tying me now, are you?'

'Should we?'

'Get out!' Colleen Richardson leapt to her feet, her fists clenched to her sides. The cat ran from the room. 'Get out! Get out!'

'Going to get gobbled up soon, I expect, Mr Yellich. We can't survive, can't compete, can't offer the breadth of service to compete with the main high street banks. But we're clinging on with our fingertips, proud to be the last independent bank

103

in England. Over three hundred years of continuous trading. Still owned by the original two founding families, the Sachses and the Lindseys. Used to be called Sachs and Lindsey's, but in a doff-the-hat to modernization, we changed our name to the Yorkshire and Lancashire Bank, and brought in those infernal machines which still make me believe all our employees spend their day watching television. Ledgers were good enough in my day. Once we had five hundred branches, now we've got fifty. Most on this side of the Pennines.' Benjamin Ffoulkes, the manager of the York branch of the Yorkshire and Lancashire Bank, was a portly man with a handlebar moustache, a yellow waistcoat and a maroon-coloured suit. He sat in a swivel chair in front of a huge wooden desk in an office of panelled wood, with velvet curtains, maroon to match his suit, held back from covering the sash windows with tasselled cords, yellow to match his waistcoat. A grandfather clock stood majestically in the corner of the room, ticking softly. Yellich found it had a quarter jack and so chimed every fifteen minutes. 'We quite enjoy our quaintness, Mr Yellich. We have our computers, as I've mentioned, but we have retained our atmosphere. This smells and sounds and looks like a bank of yesteryear, and we have applications for positions from many youngsters who want employment with us because of it. Our cheque books used to be as big as school exercise books but we had to standardize because retailers refused to accept them. One more nail in our coffin. But we enjoy a lot of customer loyalty, this branch particularly; there's a lot of old money in the Vale of York and that helps us to stay afloat. So a concession here and there is a price we can afford. But you've come to discuss the account of the late Mr Williams, of Bramley on Ouse?'

'Yes, sir.'

'Mmm . . .'

'A problem?'

'It's one of ethics, really.'

'Oh?'

'Well, yes, confess that in all my born days I've never come across a problem like this. Customer confidentiality is one thing, but if the customer is deceased, as is his wife; and I have not yet had the necessary notices, copy of the death certificate, or notification from his solicitor confirming his next of kin, I don't know whether I can help. But, if the police seek to apprehend the perpetrator of this dreadful deed, then I feel obliged . . . you know I do want to help, Mr Yellich, I really do.'

'It is a double murder.'

'It's that that makes me want to help. I confess I felt bowled over when I read of the murders in the *Post*. And I suppose you could come back with a warrant?'

'We could.'

'In a sense that would make it easier for me. The decision would be out of my hands, you see.'

'Time is of the essence, Mr Ffoulkes. If it makes it easier, we don't actually believe that money was at the root of this murder, but money has a way of shadowing all of us, our financial affairs are a profile of our lives.'

'Yes . . .' Ffoulkes smiled. 'I rather like that. Tell you what, young man, I'll offer a compromise.'

'Oh, yes?'

'I'm familiar with the account. I'll answer questions but I won't allow you access to his file, not without a warrant.'

'Fair enough.'

'Well, in the first place, please think of a child's balloon.'

'A what?'

'A child's balloon, just like those out there in the street, all the street entertainers entertaining the trippers. Good for local business, keep the street full of tourists, that's what I say. But a balloon, new, smooth, limp. Suddenly it gets inflated, then is allowed to deflate, then it's limp and wrinkled.'

'Yes?'

'That, in a nutshell, is Max Williams's account. You know the source of all the seed money, all venture capital, all start-up loans in the Vale over the last ten years has been one account.'

'Max Williams's.'

'Yes. In one. He let it flood out, haemorrhage isn't the word. But before it deflated it had to inflate.'

'He came into money?'

'Yes. Suddenly and magnificently. From his brother, I believe.'

'About how much?'

'Off the top of my head, it was about six.'

'Six? Thousand, hundred thousand?'

'Million. Six million pounds.'

The quarter jack on the grandfather clock chimed, allowing time for Yellich to recover his jaw.

'He came from nowhere.' Ffoulkes smiled, and Yellich could tell that he was enjoying his obvious surprise. 'Just a building society account and a pinkish current account with the Midland or the National Westminster. He walked in with a cheque and almost caused the cashier to faint, asked to open an account. We told him we needed time to follow up references, which we did. No bad news came and so we welcomed him with all the warmth which you can buy with six million pounds. This was some ten years ago.'

'Which is a lot of warmth, especially ten years ago.'

'Sat here in this room, drinking my last bottle of vintage claret, spent the time doing my best to persuade him to invest it, or at least put it in a deposit account, but he wanted a current account.'

'Silly man.'

'That's kind of you. Confess, Mr Yellich, I had cause to regret the sacrifice of my last bottle of vintage claret. Very rapidly did I form the opinion that I was in the company of a fool. And you know what they say about a fool and his money?'

Yellich nodded. 'I do that, sir.'

'Well, no sooner had the balloon inflated than it began to deflate. It was depressing to watch, but it's his money . . . I mean, properly invested that six million pounds would have grossed another six million in those ten years, but all the balloon did was to deflate. All Max Williams was interested in was writing cheques. Settled some money on his children, a miserly sum in proportion . . . about ten thousand each, spent

106

the rest on himself and did so foolishly. He bought a rambling but rotten eighteenth-century mansion in a parkland, looked the part, and a Rolls Royce to go with it. He achieved the image ... the day trippers from Leeds and Sheffield and such places would drive past his house set back from the road and doubtless be reassured that the English gentry is alive and well.'

'Do you know where the money came from, sir?'

'I can find out for you.' Ffoulkes turned in his high-backed wooden swivel chair and reached for a cord which hung from the ceiling and which was flush against the wall behind him. Yellich heard a bell jangle beyond the door of the office. There was a knock on the door. 'Come.' Ffoulkes answered. A young woman entered the room, looking deferential and nervous. she wore summer clothes, but of an earlier era, with heavy but comfortable-looking shoes. 'Fiona.' Ffoulkes spoke in a pleasant but fatherly manner.

'Yes, Mr Ffoulkes?'

'Can you look up the Williams account, Max Williams. You know the account I mean, he and his lady wife being recently deceased.'

'Yes, Mr Ffoulkes.'

'It was opened about ten years ago on receipt of a cheque payable to Mr Williams, drawn on the account of a firm of solicitors. Can you find out who that firm was?'

'Certainly, sir.' Fiona turned smartly and left the room.

Ffoulkes and Yellich sat in silence, broken eventually by Ffoulkes, who asked if Yellich was a married man.

'Yes, sir,' Yellich beamed. 'One son.'

'Good man. How old is he?'

'Twelve.'

'Nice age. Getting a bit full of himself, is he? A bit cocksure? Mine all did at that age. I gave out most of my good hidings when they were between nine and twelve, about. As I recall.'

'Well, he is a bit of a handful, but not so much a management problem. He's got special needs.'

'Oh, I'm sorry.'

'Well, you know, I'm not, Mr Ffoulkes. There's no denying that we were disappointed when we realized that he wasn't going to be prime minister one day, but now we feel a sense of privilege . . . a world previously unknown to us is opening up that we would not have otherwise encountered . . . and Jeremy is such a sincere, genuine person . . . he's growing up more slowly, he's hanging around that age which is a lovely age for all parents.'

Ffoulkes smiled warmly.

'We've been told that with love, and care, and stimulation and stability he could achieve a mental age of about twelve by the time he's twenty or twenty-five. And he could live in a hostel where he'll have his own room and cook his own meals if he wants to but staff will always be there, and prepared meals will be available if he wants them.'

'There is that provision then?'

'Oh, yes. And it means that we'll be a little out of the mainstream of life. We won't have grandchildren, but where Jesemy has led us and what he's given us is not at all unpleasant.'

'Good . . . good.'

There was a tap on the door. Ffoulkes said, 'Come?'

Fiona entered and handed Ffoulkes a slip of paper. 'The information you wanted, Mr Ffoulkes.'

'Thank you, Fiona,' Ffoulkes said as she turned to leave the office. Then to Yellich he said, 'Ibbotson, Utley and Swales, solicitors, Malton. Mmm. Names as solidly Yorkshire as you'll find anywhere. Do you know the origin of your name, Mr Yellich?'

'Don't, confess, Mr Ffoulkes. Eastern European, but it's been altered over the generations.'

'As it would, I daresay.'

'But back to Mr Williams.' Yellich wrote the name of the firm of solicitors on his notepad. 'Was there any pattern to the spending?'

'Foolish, ill-advised . . . more than generous . . . but the strange thing is that I don't think he made any enemies.'

'That's interesting, especially for a businessman.'

'I think the answer to that is that he was not a businessman. You see, I've been in banking all my life and it has been my experience that men who are businessmen are the ones who make enemies, and the ones who go from bungalows to eighteenth-century mansions, from Volvos to Rolls Royces. Going up you make enemies, coming down you don't, not so much anyway. People on the way down make friends.'

'Friends?'

'Of the sort who will be only too pleased to help you spend your money.'

'Ah . . .'

'Are you getting to see Mr Williams now? He wasn't so much a businessman, no matter how he styled himself.' Ffoulkes grimaced and raised his eyebrows. 'He was more of a soft touch for cash. His reputation got round and he became the softest touch in the Vale of York and in ten years he blew six million pounds, with a little help from his friends, of course.'

'Of course.'

'People starting up a money-minting business that just can't fail . . . that sort of thing, just need a few thousand to launch them, and another few thousand to get them through the first quarter . . . you grasp the pattern?'

'I do. I actually feel sorry for the man.' Yellich doodled on his pad. 'You couldn't advise him?'

'No. Can't interfere and he wouldn't listen. He seemed to live in a cloud-cuckoo-land. It wasn't long ago that he sold his mansion and his Rolls Royce. Even the move to a cramped little bungalow and loss of his prestige motor car didn't seem to bring home to him the enormity of his financial loss. Only recently he came to me for a loan of some money to have a house built . . . he got his loan but only upon surrender of the deeds to his bungalow, they're in the vault. We can recover the money from his beneficiaries, so we won't lose it – the bungalow is worth more than the loan. Feel sorry for his children . . . they're not going to inherit the bungalow. But they've both got careers, they'll survive . . . they won't sink . . . but you know Mr Yellich, the only place Max and Amanda Williams were heading was the Salvation Army shelter.' Ffoulkes paused. 'Complex man.'

'Williams?'

'Yes . . . you know, I don't wish to speak ill of the dead . . .'

'Don't then. Speak accurately of them.'

Ffoulkes smiled. 'Yes . . . once I saw a side to him I didn't like. Didn't like at all. Accepted an invitation to his house . . . not what I expected . . . the bumbling, jovial, dapper Williams was a sour individual at home . . . everything in its place . . . a tyrant, I thought . . . and the tension between him and his wife, you could cut it with a knife. Their son was there, on leave from the navy. There was a lot of tension between them, cold, simmering tension . . . him and his son, him and his wife . . . son and mother . . . just an impression. But it was a strong enough impression that I didn't accept any further invitations to socialize with the family. All that vintage claret gone to waste.'

Yellich walked out of the ancient stone doorway of the Yorkshire and Lancashire Bank and into Davygate. A hot, dry day in the ancient city; the tourists in one's and two's, family groups and school parties and the noise and the colour and the spectacle of the street entertainers; the buskers, the puppeteers, the fire-eater, the man on stilts. And the beggars in the doorways.

Vibrancy.

'You know, Shored-up, I'll never fathom you. Truly I never will.'

'All part of the intrigue, Mr Hennessey, all part of the intrigue. How did you get here, car?'

'Yes.'

'I came by train. Pleasant ride from York. Especially this time of the year. Lovely countryside.' Shored-up was, Hennessey found, to be in his usual confident manner. A tweed jacket, despite the heat, a Panama hat, a white shirt, tie with crest upon it, dark flannels, brogues, all cutting a dash, an English gentleman of military bearing, by manner and appearance.

'Can't get lost, just a short walk from the railway station to the abbey.'

'And here we are.' Hennessey and Shored-up strolled around the imposing building that was Selby Abbey, a mass of light grey stone against a blue sky, planted, it had always seemed to Hennessey, on the flat green landscape.

'It's your games, Shored-up. If it's not a pub which only the devil would know existed in Doncaster, it's the junction of two minor roads in the middle of nowhere . . . or it's telephoning a public call box which turned out to be in Thirsk. Why Thirsk?'

'Same as the pub in Doncaster, which I have heard referred to as "Donny", same as the road junction, same reason as Selby Abbey . . . prying eyes, Mr Hennessey, prying eyes. If the criminal fraternity know that I give information to the boys in blue, I will be black-balled.'

'The entire criminal fraternity gives information to the boys in blue, they do it all the time.'

'Ah, but with what quality, what consistency? I am what is known as a grass. I want not my throat cut nor my body to be flung in the Ouse. The criminals in the Vale like me, Mr Hennessey, they know that with my background I offer them a touch of class.'

'Which regiment did you serve in as the adjutant?'

'The Green Howards.'

'You'd better get your act straightened, Shored-up, the last time I asked you that question the answer was the Royal Welsh Fusiliers.'

'Yes . . .' Shored-up forced a smile.

'You may impress your apprentice criminals who look to you as a father figure, but don't try it on with me. You know and I know that the only army you've been near is the Salvation Army. Your mannerisms come from hanging around hotels and the like being a keen observer of the pukka, pukka English at play and your clothes show what can be had from the charity shops for less than a good night in the pub. So don't put it on.'

'Mr Hennessey, you do me a disservice.'

'I'm coming up to retirement, Shored-up, long earned, long looked forward to and, I feel, much deserved, and you and I are going to meet on my second last day of employment.'

'We are?'

'We are. And just for my edification, for my ears and no other ears, you will tell me what you did that we don't know about: how many scams have you been involved in, how many times have you sold partnerships in the Humber Bridge Company to unsuspecting widows? Or shares in Colombian tin mines?'

'You know, I have a respect for you, Mr Hennessey, you are the only police officer to have secured a conviction against me.'

'I remember. You got five years for fraud.'

'It was, in effect, a three-year holiday in Ford open prison. On the first day they said, "If you go out, please don't cut a hole in the fence, just walk out through the gate, we won't stop you." Then I knew I was home. Got fit in the gym, read a lot . . . missed the ladies though, did miss the ladies. And the occasional glass of chilled Frascati.'

'So you have information for me?'

'Good heavens, no.' Shored-up looked and sounded shocked.

'Shored-up . . .' Hennessey stopped walking and menaced Shored-up with eye contact.

'Nothing for you, old man. What's that quaint Yorkshire expression, "nowt for nowt and damn little for sixpence". No, I've got something to sell.'

'How much?'

'At least two hundred pounds.'

'Two hundred . . . my super will not run to that.'

'He'll have to.' Shored-up continued to walk. Reluctantly, Hennessey fell in with him. 'It's worth it. I know the value of my information, my track record in these matters is good.'

'I'll give you that,' Hennessey growled.

'How much police time can be bought for two hundred pounds?'

'Not a lot.'

'About a man day when all travelling expenses and clerical and admin support are taken into account?'

'About.'

'With this information you can crack the case.'

'Which case?'

'The Williams murder case.'

'What do you know about that?'

'Two hundred pounds worth. It's worth more, but seeing as it's you, and seeing that Max Williams and I knew each other . . .'

'You did?'

'Business partners . . . Max, good man, he put up some money to fund a venture I had devised, quite a lot of money . . . would have made us both rich . . . unfortunately, while the idea was brilliant, the timing was faulty and the public just were not ready for the product and poor Max lost his money and I had to go back to taking what work I could.'

'I bet. How many Social Security numbers have you got, Shored-up?'

'Oh, more than one, a fella can't live on what the Social Security pay, oh no . . . you see, if the government would enable honest folk to live on Social Security, then honest folk wouldn't have to be dishonest in order to make ends meet. So increase benefit levels. It would be less expensive in the long run, less thieving, less police needed, less court time.'

'Never figured you for a liberal, Shored-up. You live and you learn.'

'Two hundred pounds. Times are hard. And that's cheap.'

'All right, but if it turns out to be duff, not only will it be the last bit of grass I buy from you, but I'll pull your ever expanding file and I'll nail you for something, and your feet won't touch.'

'I do enjoy a challenge, Mr Hennessey.'

'So?'

'Well, about ten years ago.'

'Ten years?'

'That's what I said.'

'Well, you know, the other day, I was talking to a fella and

113

he told me that he was talking to a fella . . . and the upshot of this is that ten years ago poor Max Williams's brother died.'

'I didn't know Max Williams had a brother.'

'Well now, I'm earning my crust already, am I not?'

'Go on.'

'Well, not only did Max Williams's brother die about ten years ago, but many and much were the questions and rumours surrounding his death.'

'Ah . . .'

'What is said is that a man who was a churchwarden, a venerable man of the Almighty, a pillar of the community in which he lived, which was out near Malton.'

'Yes, yes.'

'Well, said churchwarden saw a young man in a sports car in the vicinity of the deceased's house at about the time he died in mysterious circumstances, it could even have been the same day.'

'Yes?'

'The churchwarden saw the young man again at the funeral of the man, Marcus Williams by name.'

'A relative?'

'Probably. Young man in a naval officer's uniform.'

Hennessey shot a glance at Shored-up but said nothing.

'The real significance is that Marcus Williams was a recluse. Just wouldn't let anybody near him unless he knew them.'

Yellich returned to Micklegate Bar Police Station, choosing to walk the walls from Lendal Bridge to Micklegate Bar. He went to Hennessey's office and tapped the door frame, the door being ajar, Hennessey at his desk with furrowed brows.

'You look worried, boss.'

'It'll keep. How did you get on?'

'Went into a time warp. Apart from the size of their cheque books and the computers, the Yorkshire and Lancashire Bank belongs to a different era, Bakelite telephones, bell pulls to summon the staff . . . tell you, Dr D'Acre would be at home there.'

'What do you mean, Yellich?'

114

'Well, her and that old car she runs . . .'

'You do her a disservice; she told me once that "that old car she runs", was her father's first and only car, he cherished it, she loved him, when he died she clung on to it. Has it looked after by a small independent garage, the proprietor and mechanics drool over the machine and the proprietor has won her promise to let him have first refusal if she ever comes to sell it.'

'Guarantees good service, if nothing else.'

'Cynicism doesn't really become you, Yellich. How did you get on?'

'Well, in a nutshell, Mrs Richardson doesn't really have an alibi. Says she was in Ireland over the last weekend but can't prove it.'

'How convenient for her.'

'Max Williams, according to his bank manager, inherited six million pounds ten years ago and blew the lot. Inherited it from his brother who lived . . .'

'Near Malton.'

'Yes, how did you know that, boss?'

Hennessey told Yellich about his meeting with Shored-up. He glanced at the clock on the wall. 'Tomorrow, I want you to drive out to Malton.'

7

Friday

. . . in which Sergeant Yellich probes a poignant life.

Yellich drove from York to Malton through the rich country-
side of North Yorkshire. It was, he reflected, rich in many
ways, rich in terms of nature's bounty, and he felt indeed
fortunate to be living and working in this part of the world.
And it was rich in terms of the wealth of the folk who live
here. Here is old farming money, as evinced by large houses
set back from the road, of John Deeres in the field, of Mercedes
Benz and Range Rovers parked outside grocery stores. The
area between York and Malton is an area where the main
roads are narrow and not heavily occupied with traffic, of
villages which give the impression of having changed little
in the last two or three generations, of gently undulating
landscape, a patchwork of fields under corn, of green pasture,
of darker green woodland. Yellich entered Malton, located
the police station and parked in a 'police only' parking bay,
leaving a yellow 'police' sticker on his windscreen.

Later, sitting at a vacant desk over a hospitable cup of coffee,
with a warm invitation to help himself to further cups, and
enjoying the calm of Malton Police Station, he settled back
and read the file about the death of Marcus Williams, some
ten years previous.

Marcus Williams, it had been recorded, had lived for many
years at Oakfield House, Little Asham, Malton. A young
officer who was clearly destined to go far in the police had

compiled the report and had put much detail into it. Oakfield House, he had recorded, was a seven-bedroomed mansion dating from the early nineteenth century and stood in five acres of grounds, which were all that remained of the original estate. The officer had further revealed his dedication to his career by providing not just a detailed description of Oakfield House, but a map as well, hand drawn, but neat, as if lifted from rough workings, which showed that Oakfield House was geographically remote. It was not so much in Little Asham, rather that was the nearest village. It probably, thought Yellich, stood within the ancient parish boundary of Little Asham, but only just. He saw that to reach Oakfield House, he had to take a minor road from Malton towards Asham-on-the-hill, then to proceed to the village of Great Asham, beyond which was Little Asham, and beyond which, at the end of an unadopted road, stood Oakfield House. The distance between Malton Police Station/Post Office, the alternative centres of any town, and Oakfield House, was given as seven miles: approx.

Marcus Williams lived alone at Oakfield House. He had a caretaker and a gardener, both of whom attended 'near daily', and both lived in Little Asham. Their addresses were recorded and Yellich took a note of them.

Of the death itself, it was recorded that Mrs O'Shea had found the deceased Marcus Williams drowned in his bath. It was noted that the death, whilst not suspicious in itself, was curious, because Marcus Williams was known to favour showers, and was not known to take baths. On this occasion he had and it appeared to have cost him his life. It was strange, Yellich thought, that an open verdict should be recorded because there was no sign of any other hand in the affair. It was a man who lived alone, drew a bath, fell asleep and drowned. About ten people a year die in such a manner in the United Kingdom. It seemed to Yellich that an open verdict in this case was an unduly cautious verdict. There seemed to him no reason to return a verdict which in lay speak means 'here we are not told the whole story'. But he read on.

Of the man himself, it was recorded that he was a recluse who would not let anyone near him unless he knew and trusted them. He had amassed a fortune on the stock exchange, by consulting the *Financial Times* each day, telephoning his stockbroker if he thought fit, and conducting all other business via his solicitors, Ibbotson, Utley and Swales of Malton. If a document needed to be signed, a representative of the firm would visit him. It was also recorded, almost as a footnote, that Marcus Williams stood just over three feet tall, suffering as he did from cretinism.

Yellich closed the file and handed it to the duty sergeant.

'Got all you want, sir?' The duty sergeant signed for the file.

'Not sure,' said Yellich. 'Not sure at all. I think I'd like to visit the house itself. Who lives there now?'

'Oh my, bane of our lives, thorn in our side.'

'A rock star?'

'I wish it was. No, all I can say is that it's now inhabited, and that's the only word I can use, inhabited by a team of weirdos who call themselves "the World Union of God"'

'Ah, ha . . . a cult. You've got problems.'

'One we've got to live with. Seems to me it consists of a lot of young people in robes who look very lost and needy.' The portly duty sergeant shook his head slowly. 'Occasionally we used to see them in the streets with a gaily painted covered wagon pulled by a cow, asking for "alms", as they put it. Don't seem to do that now. A local journalist did some digging and found out that the World Union of God is American-based, its guru, who has some fancy name, lives with his female acolytes in a "temple" in California, and has a sacred chariot which sounded to the journalist to be very similar to a Lear jet. They pay in money to the local banks here which is credited to an account in Geneva. But they have a font of knowledge in the form of a tree in India which is in permanent bloom and which only their guru in his private jet and one or two acolytes can visit. So they say.'

'Been here before, methinks.'

'Aye . . . but they're open and honest enough, you can walk up to the gate and ask to be shown round. We're satisfied that they've nothing to hide, they're just a bit soft in the head and are wasting valuable years, if you ask me.'

'Well, I'll go and have a chat with them. If I don't come back, send a search party for me.'

'Will do, sir.' The sergeant smiled.

Yellich drove out of Malton into steadily closing country-side, until he came to a narrow lane which had once, many years earlier, been metalled, now it was cratered after many years of ice and rain action. He drove gingerly, trying, not always successfully, to avoid the potholes. The foliage on either side was close, overwhelmingly so. He came to two large stone gateposts with wrought-iron gates which were held shut with a heavy padlock and chain. A painted sign on the gate showed a robed, Christ-like figure with outstretched palms against a celestial background, standing above the planet earth, with the Americas dead central to the planet as it was depicted. A brass bell, similar to a ship's bell, was fastened to the gate. Yellich got out of his car and rang the bell loudly, causing the birds in the nearby trees and bushes to take to flight. There was no response, and calm and tranquillity, birdsong and insect chirruping returned.

Yellich waited for a minute, perhaps, he thought, nearer two, then he rang the bell again, and again birds in the nearby greenery took to flight.

Still no response.

Then a robed figure, a male, approached the gate from within the grounds. He wore a long white robe, sandals, and walked with his hands crossed in front of him. He walked up to the gate and held eye contact with Yellich. He had a calm manner, his skin was clean, very clean, as though the pores had been cleaned by steam, Turkish-bath style. His eyes had a glazed expression which unnerved Yellich. 'Can I help you, my brother?' he said softly. Yellich thought the man to be the same age as himself.

'Police.' Yellich showed his ID. The man made to reach through the bars of the gate to get hold of the plastic card but Yellich withdrew it. 'No, you can look at it but you can't hold it, that's the rule.'

'Very well. What can I do for you, my brother?'

'I'd like to look inside the house.'

'Why?'

'Police business.'

'You have some concern about the house?'

'No, nor about you or your friends. It concerns a matter which took place before you took up occupancy. I want to examine the scene of an accident.'

'Well, we have nothing to hide and welcome all visitors.' The man took a key from his pocket and unlocked the padlock. He opened the gate and Yellich stepped inside. He turned and watched the man lock the gate behind him. The man turned to Yellich. 'We have nothing to hide and welcome visitors, but we do like to control egress and exit, it's no more than you keeping your front door locked.'

'Fair enough.'

'Shall we go up?' The man began to walk up the wide, curving driveway. 'We try to keep ourselves to ourselves in order not to antagonize local people but we don't succeed. When we first came here we would find padlocks and chains round the gate extra to the one we put on. We took our wagon and oxen into the community but stopped when the local children would not stop throwing stones at us. It's the nature of prejudice, people are frightened of anything that is different, anything they don't understand. You know, it amuses me that the British can get on their high horse about racism and human rights issues in other countries, but if a group of Neanderthals had escaped the march of time and still lived a Neanderthal existence in the Scots lowlands or Thetord Forest, do they honestly think the same kind of prejudice would not exist here?'

'I imagine it would,' Yellich conceded.

'It is, as I said, the nature of prejudice. How is my brother called?'

'Yellich. DS Yellich.'

'I am Pastor Cyrus. D? S? David? Simon?'

120

'Detective Sergeant.'

Pastor Cyrus, nodded and the two men walked side by side in silence up the drive and emerged from the trees into a lawned area in which stood a large house of blackened stone. Clearly, thought Yellich, early Victorian as had been reported, squat, uncompromising, very 'new money' of its day, not here is the graceful architecture of the classicism of a century earlier, here was the representation of the beginning of the sweeping aside of the English aristocracy, a process, mused Yellich, which is not yet complete. On the lawn, a group of children in robes sat cross-legged in a circle listening to a young woman, also robed, who spoke to them. Yellich noted that not one of the children, nor the young woman, even glanced at him, clearly a stranger in city clothing. He felt invisible.

'How long have you been here?'

'About seven years. We had a haven in the East of London but had to endure violence and intimidation. It was a testing time for us but eventually our leader had a vision of a large house surrounded by trees somewhere in the North of England, and I and another were sent to seek it. We found it and money was forthcoming, and Oakfield House as it was, is now "the British Temple of the World Union of God".'

'So the house had been vacant for some time before you bought it?'

'It had, and vandalized. Not a pane of glass remained intact. Village lads, you know.'

'You've made a good job of its repair.'

'I thank my brother for that comment.'

'What do you know about the last occupant?'

'Little, though doubtless it was he that sustained the accident which interests my brother?'

'He is, or was, or whatever.'

'Well, our first impression was that he was a brother of restricted growth, all the doors in the house had handless set low down, at about waist level to the average person.'

'That doesn't mean anything.' Yellich turned to Pastor Cyrus. 'That was the Victorian fashion, it just made sense

121

to have door handles which were at hand height if the adult was standing with his arms by his side. It was only in the twentieth-century that we thought it would be a good idea to put door handles at shoulder height.'

'Oh . . . but even so, there were, and still are, other indications: the sink in the kitchen, well, one of them, was lowered, there was also a small cooker very low on the ground and some wooden steps by the bath and a sort of platform in the bath on which to sit or stand. We have retained them because we find it useful for the children.'

'I'd be particularly interested to see the bathroom.'

'The bathroom with the steps and the platform? I ask because we have three bathrooms.'

'Yes, that one.'

Yellich and Pastor Cyrus approached the steps of the house and as they did so the large door with a highly polished brass handle swung open silently. A girl of about eighteen years, full white robe and sandals, hands crossed in front of her at waist height, stood in the doorway.

'This is Lamb,' said Pastor Cyrus.

Yellich smiled at Lamb, who said nothing but cast down her eyes in a gesture of humility.

'Lamb,' Pastor Cyrus addressed the girl, 'please escort our brother to the children's bathroom and also anywhere else he wishes to go.' Then he turned to Yellich. 'Lamb is a recent convert, she has been with us for only a month now and so is still a novice. Please don't ask her questions because she has taken a vow of silence which she must keep for three months, except for one hour each evening when she may ask questions of the elders as part of her training. Apart from that she may not utter at all except in an emergency.'

'So she can yell her head off if the house catches fire?'

But Pastor Cyrus simply smiled and said, 'If you'd like to follow Lamb.'

Lamb took Yellich into the cool, dark, spacious interior of the old house. In the front hall men and women, all in robes, read in silence. Lamb climbed an angled staircase and walked along a narrow corridor. In one room off the corridor,

Yellich saw rows of children sitting in front of computers with determined concentration. Not one looked up as he passed the open door of their room. Presently Lamb came to the bathroom in question, stood on one side of the door, bowed her head and with a fluid wrist action, bade him enter the room.

So this, Yellich thought, as he entered the room, was where Marcus Williams died. It was a rectangular room with a deep, long bath set in the middle of the floor, as was often the style in Victorian houses – it was a bathroom, so let the bath dominate it. A shower attachment, obviously of much later design, was fastened to a stainless-steel support, very barrack-room basic. It would not have lasted long if the house had had a woman to organize it, but it would, thought Yellich, suit the functional, no-frills needs of a bachelor. He noted the wooden steps leading up to the bath which were not attached but could be set apart if necessary, and a seat or a platform in the bath which was of wood and suspended from the sides. It was about three feet wide, and so, thought Yellich, more probably a platform for a person taking a shower, than an infirm person sitting on it rather than fully in the bath. Yellich turned to Lamb and said, 'Thank you. I've seen enough.'

Outside, Pastor Cyrus stood motionless in the sun, awaiting his return. Yellich stepped out of the cool of the building and into the heat. 'Computers?' he said.

'This is not an archaic church, brother Yellich. God wants us to keep up with His times.'

'I liked him.' Sam Sprie sat in an upright chair outside the front door of his small council house. Yellich sat beside him in a white plastic chair which had been brought from the rear garden for him. They sipped tea which had been pressed on them by an insistent Mrs Sprie who had then departed dutifully into the shade of her home, behind a multicoloured fly screen in the form of many thin strips of plastic which hung on the door of the house, not a permanent fixture, but put up and taken down as the need arose. The garden in front of Sam Sprie's house was a sea of multicoloured flowers, mainly pansies, boarded by a small privet hedge, neatly trimmed, green at either side, yellow at the front. It was a gardener's garden. 'I hardly ever saw him.'

'You hardly ever saw him, yet you liked him?'

'That's why I liked him. He allowed me to get on with my job and didn't interfere, you can always tell whether your gardener's working. So long as I shut the gates behind me, as Mrs O'Shea had to as well. We both had a key to the padlock on the front gate so we could let ourselves in in the morning and lock up behind us after we left for the day.'

'So there was just Mr Williams in the house each evening?'

'Each evening and each weekened. Mrs O'Shea and myself worked five days a week. Mr Williams could cook a meal if he had to, so he didn't starve when Mrs O'Shea was ill, or on holiday, or each weekend. But no, he wasn't alone strictly speaking, he had three Dobermans. He was safe, allright, the Dobermans knew me and Mrs O'Shea and Mr Williams but practically nobody else. The post was left in a box by the gate, as was the milk. The Dobermans would protect him, at least buy him enough time to phone the police.'

'And how would the police get through the gate and past the dogs?'

Sprie smiled and nodded his head. 'Don't think he thought of that. He was a bit like those people who barricade their homes against burglars, which is all very well until you want to get out to escape the fire. Bars keep them out, but they also keep you in. But that was Mr Williams. A little . . . what's the word?'

'Eccentric?'

'Aye, that as well.'

'What sort of man was he?'

'Better ask Mrs O'Shea that, she knew him better than I did. Like I said, if the garden was kept he never bothered me. I never saw him, save in passing, never went into Oakfield House.'

'He drowned in the bath?'

'You asking me or telling me?'

'Asking.'

'Aye . . . well, there's some as says he did and some as says he didn't.'

'Meaning?'

'Well, his death just didn't seem right . . . he never took baths but I didn't know that until after he died. Mrs O'Shea . . . she'll . . .'

'Aye . . . I'll ask her.

'He lived alone. A recluse?'

'That's the word. I've been thinking of him as a hermit but the word didn't fit . . . recluse . . . yes, I like that word.'

'No visitors at all?'

'One or two over the years, a tall man would visit once in a while. I was told that was Mr Williams's brother . . . first time I saw him he drove up in a car with a wife and a couple of children . . . I was close by that time . . . he went into the house looking worried, made the children and his wife wait in the car a good long while. Then came out looking pleased with himself, I saw him smile at his wife and tap his wallet . . . you know, his jacket breast pocket. His wife smiled back. Then they drove off.'

'What do you think had happened?'

'He tapped him for some money. That's what I felt. Since then I've only ever had the impression of the brother visiting Mr Williams whenever he wanted money. Nothing regular about the visits . . . I mean, I've got one surviving brother and we see each other at the Sun each Sunday lunchtime. It was nothing like that, Mr Williams's brother would visit as and when and stay for about half an hour then he'd not visit again for three, four months, then he'd turn up and leave again as though he'd got what he wanted. Didn't take to him. Mrs O'Shea told me that Mr Williams was upset that his brother had kept his wife and children in the car when they visited that first time, he felt as if his brother was ashamed of him.'

'Ashamed?'

'Well, Mr Williams, he was about that high.' Sam Sprie held a sinewy arm out level about three feet from the concrete path on which he and Yellich's chairs stood.

'Was he self-conscious about it?'

'Well, if he was, his brother hiding him from his sister-in-law and nephew and niece didn't help, especially when the only reason they visited was to tap him for cash.'

'It wouldn't. I'm surprised he entertained his brother at all.'

'He was a generous sort. He had a lake in the grounds.'

'A lake?'

'Very big pond, very small lake . . . it was circular, about from here to that tree from bank to bank.' Sprie pointed to a magnificent oak tree in a field opposite the line of council houses. Yellich thought the distance between house and tree to be about two hundred yards.

'Big enough.'

'It was about ten feet deep with steep sides, it was excavated by the man who had Oakfield House built back in the eighteen-thirties. He created the lake and had it stocked with trout. Anyway, the lake hadn't been fished for a while before Mr Williams moved in and when he moved in it was just teeming with fish. We were looking over the grounds after he'd taken me on and he told me he wanted the lake filled in. I asked him if we could take the fish, we have an angling club in the village . . . he said yes . . . we organized ourselves, no more than six rods at any one time, each man having a four-hour slot . . . and still it took us a week to fish out the lake. He was generous like that, but that week sticks in my mind because there were more folk in the grounds than ever before or since, and in that week I never saw Mr Williams once. But he was accepted well after that, people knew about him, and left him alone . . . not like the group of weirdos that are in there now . . . we don't know what's going in the house, aye.'

'Any other visitors that you recall?'

'Only one, a young man, called a few times . . . this was in the last year of Mr Williams's life . . . a friend, a relative . . . I got the impression that he was calling on Mr Williams, not his money . . . he also liked the dogs and they took to him after a while . . . throwing sticks for them. He was seen in the village at about the time Mr Williams died. Not by me, by Sydney Tamm. He used to be the churchwarden at St Mark's.'

'Used to be?'

'He's still alive . . .'

'Where do I find him?'

'Ask at the vicarage. That's St Mark's.' Sprie pointed to a steeple, dark grey against the blue sky. 'The vicarage is behind the church. The vicar will put you right.'

'I used to enjoy doing for Mr Williams.' Tessie O'Shea sat in an armchair with a black cat on her lap. 'Just me and Petal now, isn't it, Petal? You know, you get to an age when all you can do is enjoy each day for its own sake and not worry too much about the future.' Tessie O'Shea's cottage was small and cosy and warm and homely. As much as Sam Sprie's garden had been a gardener's garden, Yellich thought that Tessie O'Shea's cottage was a domestic worker's domicile. It was a stone-built structure with thick stone walls which Yellich knew would be warm in the winter when the open hearth was burning and he noted it to be cool in the summer. The stonework above the door of the cottage had a date 1676 AD carved into it and it sobered Yellich to ponder that when Napoleon retreated from Moscow Mrs O'Shea's cottage was already in excess of two hundred and thirty years old. 'But you want to know about Mr Williams?'

'Yes. Huge house for you to look after.'

'If he lived in all of it, it would have been, but he had the one bedroom, the one sitting room, the one study, he ate in the kitchen. The rest of the house gathered dust. So I could manage it. You know when I said he used to eat in the kitchen, I meant that he sat down with me and ate at the kitchen table, me and him ate together, him in his high chair . . . what kind of man would sit down and eat with his domestic? A gentleman would, that's who would. He was a gentleman, treated me as an equal. I loved working for him. I did better for him because of it . . . his attitude, I mean. I always made sure he had plenty of tinned food in so he could survive if I wasn't there, so he didn't have to go out to the shops. He was a bit shy about his height, he was a small man, about three feet high. It wasn't so bad when I was ill for a day or two, or at the weekends, but I used to enjoy a fortnight in Ramsgate every July. I'd worry about him then.'

'I understand that it was yourself who found his body?'

'Aye . . . me . . . I'll never forget it . . . I knew something was wrong . . . the dogs, you see, they were in a strange state . . . looking sorrowful . . . whimpering . . . and they flocked round me when I rode up on my bicycle . . . as if I was a rescuer. I went into the house . . . the dogs had licked their water and food bowls dry . . . so I gave them some water, plenty of water . . . it was the summertime, this time of year . . . and then went looking for Mr Williams . . . calling out his name . . . found him in the bath . . . his little body and all that water. Face down, he was. There's a few things that didn't add up, oh no, they didn't, didn't add up at all.'

'Such as?'

'Well, for one thing he didn't take baths. He had a fear of drowning, he had the lake in the grounds filled in for that reason, pretty well the first thing he did was to fill in the lake.'

'Sam Sprie has just told me, he let the angling club fish it out, and then filled it in.'

'Yes . . . that's right . . . the village liked him after that . . . but those people that have got the house now . . . but anyway, he always took showers, had a platform built to stand on . . . he had the shower put up for him, bit of a contraption but it worked. Then he had some steps built up to get from the floor onto the platform. The bath was a bit big for him to get into . . . you imagine a bath . . .'

'Yes.'

'The rim of which is just below shoulder height as you stand against it, if you're in it and outstretch your arms, you can touch either side, just, and if you stand at the opposite end of the bath to the taps, it takes you half a dozen full-length strides, at least, to reach the taps . . . well, that was the size

128

of the bath for Mr Williams. I can see why he was frightened of drowning.'

'So can I, since you put it like that.'

'And when I found him, the steps and the platform were up against the wall, well away from the bath . . . he couldn't have got into the bath without the steps . . .'

'Are you suggesting someone else was involved?'

'I'm not suggesting anything, but . . . well, this is going back ten years now . . . but the bath was filled with tap water.'

Yellich raised his eyebrows as if to say, What other sort of water is there?

'I mean,' said Mrs O'Shea. 'I mean as opposed to water from the shower. The taps on the bath were never used, they hadn't been used at all during the time that Mr Williams was the owner. The house was empty for a while before Mr Williams moved in . . . they'd rusted shut . . . I couldn't turn them on, I used the water from the shower when I cleaned the bath. I don't say they were rusted solid, a strong man could have turned them on, but I couldn't, and Mr Williams didn't. But when I found him, the shower was dry, not dripping, because Mr Williams never turned it off properly, but the taps were dripping. And I turned them on and then off again, easily, they'd been freed off.'

'Hence the open verdict,' Yellich said more to himself than Mrs O'Shea.

'Probably. There was something deliberate about the death, but I don't think anybody wanted to say suicide . . . no note or anything . . . Mr Williams wasn't depressed . . . he was just trotting along with life and had a good sense of humour . . . I mean, he didn't like being a cretin, he told me once that that was his medical condition . . . I've heard the word being used as an insult, I never knew it was a real medical condition until I met Mr Williams, but he just accepted it . . . his dogs didn't see him as a dwarf. The gardener never saw him from one week to the next, he had few visitors . . . there was just me . . . and after a while, after a short while, I didn't see him as different at all. I got to like doing for him, as I said. Used to talk to me, tell me how he'd done on the stock market . . .

"Did well today, Mrs O'Shea," he'd say or, "Didn't do too well, but I'll make it up tomorrow." Then he'd spend time with his dogs, he loved them and they loved him . . . didn't take them walks but they had the run of the grounds. He just wasn't a suicide type person. There was nothing to do with the dogs after he died but have them put down. They pined for him . . . they wouldn't be taken from the house . . . I know what they felt . . . I gave up my work after that and settled for my pension and my savings. I just couldn't do for anybody after Mr Williams.'

'Did you ever meet his relatives?'

'His brother once or twice, Mr Max Williams, smooth type, gold fillings . . . all smiles and daggers . . . he visited once and left his wife and children in the car outside the house on a hot day . . . after that he just visited alone. One day . . . well, see, if you "do" for a man or a family long enough you get to know what's going on and once Mr Williams told me that his brother was getting expensive, then he said, "but what can I do? Blood is blood." That's what he said. "Blood is blood."'

'Did you meet his nephew or niece?'

'The nephew. The navy man. Arrogant giant of a man. The way he looked at me . . . like dirt. He called me "O'Shea" and he called the gardener "Sprie", just surnames . . . but never in Mr Williams's hearing. He was handsome in his uniform and he knew it, very full of himself. I suppose the girls would go for him. Visited Mr Williams a few times in the last eighteen months . . . spent time with the dogs . . . bought them liquorice . . . dogs are fond of liquorice . . . walking the grounds with them. They got to wagging their tails when he came.'

'One last question, Mrs O'Shea, the day you found Mr Williams's body. What day of the week was it, can you recall?'

'It was a Monday. Definitely a Monday. It'll be written up, you'll be able to check it, but I can tell you it was a Monday. First day of the week, last day of my working life.'

Yellich walked the short, but not unpleasant, walk to the

vicarage which was not, to his surprise, a stone-built, ivy-covered house, but a newly built semi-detached house set in a neat garden and a gravel drive. He thought himself fortunate to find the Reverend Eaves at home. He revealed himself to be a tall, kindly seeming, silver-haired man and was pleased to direct Yellich to the home of Sydney Tamm who had been churchwarden at the time of Marcus Williams's death.

Sydney Tamm was by contrast a short man with a furrowed brow. He drove the garden fork into the ground between the row of potato plants in his front garden and looked at Yellich. 'Police?'

'Aye.'

'About?'

'Marcus Williams.'

'Aye. Sitting up and taking notice at last, are you?'

'Should we?'

'Aye. Mind, I can't tell you anything that's not known, isn't known . . . well, you'd better come into the house.'

The closest description that Yellich could find to describe Sydney Tamm's house was 'refuse tip'. It even smelled like one. The accumulated tabloids revealed that it probably hadn't been cleaned for the last five years. The house was probably difficult to live in in the winter but the summer heat made the smell near unbearable to Yellich. Many flies buzzed in the window or flew in figure-of-eight patterns in the air above the table on which remnants of food remained on dirty plates, themselves on newspaper which served as a tablecloth.

'I'm not proud of my house. I'm not ashamed of it.' Tamm sat in an armchair. 'You can sit in that chair there, if you want, but most of my visitors choose to stand.'

'I'll stand.'

'Suit yourself.' Tamm reached for a packet of cigarettes, and taking one, lit it with a match, putting the spent match back in the box. 'She'd turn in her grave if she could see her house.' He nodded to a photograph of a bonny-looking woman which stood, in a frame, on the mantelpiece.

'You were the churchwarden of St Mark's?'

'Was. Don't qualify . . . not a Christian any more, am I? Can you imagine a Christian living in a house like this? Cleanliness is next to godliness. I had religion all my days, and then my Myrtle took cancer . . . if there was a God, He wouldn't have let a good woman like her suffer like she did. I buried her decent like, but then I told the vicar I wanted no more of his cant. I spend my days down the Dunn Cow now with the rest of the old lads of the village . . . it's the only pub around here for the fogies, all the rest is for the young 'un's, all that music, them machines with their weird sound and the flashing lights. But the Cow, it's still as a pub should be.'

'You don't use the Sun with the angling club?'

Tamm looked at Yellich, as if surprised at his knowledge of Little Asham. 'No . . . no, I don't use the Sun.' Said as if there was a story . . . a fall-out with the publican, a row with the anglers. Something had happened. 'The Cow's all right and all those boys who have never had religion have all been right all along, and the vicar and me have been wrong all along. The vicar, he calls from time to time, but less so now, he's giving up on me . . . his lost sheep is gone . . . devoured by the wolf at the Dunn Cow.'

'I'm sorry.'

'The smell is terrible.'

'It's not so bad, a good clean, plenty of disinfectant, you could get on top of your house again in no time.'

'Cancer. The smell of cancer. It's a terrible smell. It's one of those smells . . . smell it once and you'll never forget it . . . it stays in your nose. Myrtle . . . she had it on her skin . . . started out as a mole . . . then it was all over in the end, all over her. Her skin looked like . . . poor Myrtle . . . even now, five years this November, I can still smell the smell. I sleep downstairs, the smell hasn't left the room where she died. Not properly . . . I won't open a window, nor the door. Do you want to go up and smell it?'

'No . . . I don't think so.'

'If you did, you'll never go near those canting priests and their steeple houses again.'

'Again, all I can say is I'm sorry.'

'Aye . . . look, I don't get my pension for a day or two, I

132

don't suppose you could let me have the money for a beer, only there's a darts match at the Cow?'

Yellich took his wallet out and laid a ten-pound note on the sideboard. 'Tenner OK?'

'Thanks . . . I can go out tonight.'

'So, Mr Williams?'

'Aye, there's still rumours about yon. I saw a young man driving through the village on the day he died, the Sunday. I'd locked up the church after Evensong, that would be at seven-thirty. I was walking home when the car passed me, going quite fast for the narrow road. Saw the driver, young man . . .'

'He was driving away from Oakfield House?'

'Yes. He came to the village and took the York road. It goes through Malton, but if he was going to the coast, there's another road he'd take which would avoid Malton. It's a fair bet he was heading to York, in that direction, anyway. I didn't recognize him, he was a stranger. But I saw him just once again . . . he was a mourner at Mr Williams's funeral; being a churchwarden, I was at the funeral . . . making sure everything was where it ought to be, and he was there, same young man, then he was in a naval officer's uniform.'

Yellich returned to Malton, and parking his car in front of the police station, ensuring that the 'police' sign was in the windscreen, he set off on foot, seeking the firm of Ibbotson, Utley and Swales. He amused himself by looking for it, rather than enquiring as to its location. Exercising logic, and the benefit of previous observation, he confined his search to the older part of Malton where he found one solicitors' office, then another, then an estate agent's, then beyond that, the building occupied by the firm of Ibbotson, Utley and Swales.

'Our juniors never let up, not allowed to.' Julian Ibbotson reclined in his chair in an oak-panelled room which reminded Yellich of Ffoulkes's office in the Yorkshire and Lancashire Bank in York, the same solid, timeless quality. 'Every ten minutes has to be accounted for. Not like that when I started,

I doubt I could stand the pace. I belong to a different era, thank goodness. Too fast-paced for me, even in sleepy Malton. Retirement beckons, oh my, how it beckons.'

'You have plans for your retirement, sir?'

'Oh yes . . . plans, plans and yet more plans. But enough, I understand that you wish to see me about a client of ours?'

'Ex-client. Marcus Williams.'

'Oh yes . . . Oakfield House, open verdict . . . eight, ten years ago?'

'That's the one.'

'If you want to access the documents you'll need a warrant, but I wish to help and so I'll answer any questions as accurately as I can.'

'Why do you wish to help?'

'The open verdict. I'm a lawyer, you are a police officer, we both know what an open verdict means.' Ibbotson smiled, a thin smile from a long face.

'A piece of the puzzle is missing?'

'Yes . . . his death was no accident, he wasn't the suicidal type . . . he had a physical condition which may, nay, certainly *would* have taken some coming to terms with, but once he'd made the adjustment he had a lot to live for. Foul pay cannot be ruled out.'

'It can't?'

'And a police officer from York, not our local branch of the North Yorkshire Constabulary, what, I ask myself is this to do with the double murder of Mr and Mrs Williams of which I read all agog in the *Yorkshire Post* a day or two ago?'

'Much,' said Yellich. 'Possibly. We are pursuing a line of enquiry, more than one, in fact. Can I ask you who benefited from Mr Marcus Williams's estate?'

'His brother. The now also deceased Mr Max Williams.'

'Quite a sum was involved?'

'About six million pounds. And that was after death duties. Later he came into another half-million pounds when Oakfield House was sold to those who have come to save us. They and their oxen.'

'Yes . . .'

'Confess I'm more than a little surprised that Mr Max Williams should be living in such a modest bungalow when he died. I saw the photograph in the *Post* and I nearly fell off my chair. Can you tell me if it was by choice or necessity that he lived in such a small house?'

'Necessity.'

'That takes skill.' Ibbotson fixed Yellich with steely eyes. 'Getting rid of six million pounds in ten years is an act of consummate skill.'

'Any other beneficiaries?'

'Scanner appeal at the hospital in York, plus a charity for disabled persons, quite generous, I suppose, in comparison to the usual donations they receive, but neither sum made a dent in his estate.'

'What about his niece and nephew?'

'I didn't know he had a niece and nephew and thereby I answer your question. All went to his brother, save a hundred thousand to the scanner appeal and a similar amount to the disabled persons charity.'

As he drove back to York, Louise D'Acre entered Yellich's mind. He had always seen the Home Office pathologist as being headmistressy in a prim and stuffy sort of way, driving the old Riley as if fashion and modernity didn't reach her, yet all the time she had been cherishing her father's memory by nurturing his one and only motor car so that it still gave sterling service long after its design life had expired. Frightening, he thought, frightening how you can be wrong about people.

8

Friday

*. . . In which Chief Inspector Hennessey lunches with the Senior
Service and afterwards pays a house call.*

'I'm only prepared to speak off the record.'

'Fair enough,' grunted Hennessey.

'Good.' The man paused. 'Well, there's a pub in the village near the base, the Dog and Duck, they do a pass-
able ploughman's lunch. Shall we say between twelve and
twelve-thirty?'

'Excellent, thank you, sir. I'll be there.' Hennessey replaced
the receiver gently. Suddenly Patrick Wood came to mind . . .
Patrick, of course . . . a good bloke, a very good bloke. One
more name for the list. He spent the remainder of the morning
addressing administrative matters and at eleven-thirty, signed
out and drove out towards Knaresborough where he located
HMS Halley and the village, and finally the Dog and Duck.

'Mr Hennessey?' Commander Timmins revealed himself
to be a short man, bespectacled, with a grey suit and white
shirt with blue stripes and a dark-blue tie, black shoes. He
approached Hennessey confidently as Hennessey entered the
pub, lowering his head against the low beams.

'That's me.' The two men shook hands. Each ordered a
ham ploughman's and each a pint of Black Sheep Best. They
carried their beer to a table in a bay window composed of
many small panes of glass. 'Nice pub.'

'Don't use it often.' Timmins sipped his beer. 'It's the policy

136

of all military bases not to use pubs in the immediate location of the base. It means we don't dominate the local area in the way that university students dominate their local area, keeps the relationship within the local community more positive than would otherwise be the case. We don't allow our boys or girls to drink in groups of four or more less than four miles from the base. We call it the "fours rule". It means that our impact is dissolved over a wider area. But a one-off in mufti, as you see, that's not against the rules.'

'Well, thanks for seeing me. It may or may not come to nothing, but it concerns Lieutenant Williams.'

'Yes?'

'His parents have been murdered.'

'I know. He's told me. He hasn't given much away, he hasn't requested compassionate leave, says he doesn't want it. He says the job keeps his mind occupied and by fortunate coincidence he was based close to home when tragedy struck. Even in today's shrinking navy, he could still have been anywhere in the world, even as a shore-based officer, yet when tragedy strikes his family, he is based within three hours' walk of his parents' house.'

'Coincidence, as you say.'

'He's not a suspect, I hope?'

'He has no motivation, he won't benefit from their deaths. They were broke, even their home was about to be repossessed, so we think.'

'Really? I wonder where he got it from?'

'It?'

'The money. He has only a modest salary, but has a sports car and rents accommodation off the base.'

'He's allowed to do that?'

'Oh yes, only the most junior personnel, both officers and other ranks, are kept inside the fence. But once someone has got some time in they can live off the base. So long as they report when they're expected to report, there isn't a problem. The real obstacle of living off the base is the cost of accommodation, even with the rent allowance. But money never seemed to be an obstacle to Lieutenant Williams.'

Timmins ceased speaking and both men leaned backwards as a generous ploughman's lunch was laid before each of them. Timmins smiled at the young waitress and Hennessey said, 'Thank you.

'I'll remember this pub.' Hennessey took his knife and fork from the paper napkin.

'So, Williams . . . yes, he definitely had private means, but so do my other officers. You can't afford the lifestyle that is expected of you on the salary a junior officer is paid . . . expected to put in appearances at every party, expected to contribute to parties you know you won't be attending . . .'

'Not my lifestyle. Too hectic.'

'The services are a way of life. It's either for you or it isn't.'

'I did two years in the navy.'

'Did you?' Timmins beamed. 'National Service?'

'How did you guess? Saw the world as far as Portsmouth. Didn't enjoy it but I survived. Got my ear burned for returning a salute . . . I was on duty standing at the stern of the ship, two officers came aboard and saluted in my direction.'

'Oh no!'

'Fraid so . . .' Hennessey smiled. 'So I dutifully returned the salute and got my ear burned.'

'As you would have done.'

'What officer in what navy salutes a rating! They were saluting the ensign, of course . . . but he let it go at that . . . half-witted National Serviceman . . .'

'We were not unhappy when conscription was abolished. We're much happier as a volunteer force . . . one volunteer is worth twelve pressed men . . . so what else can I tell you about Lieutenant Williams?'

'Anything and everything. He's not a suspect, but in cases like this, we like to obtain as broad a picture as possible. We have two suspects in the frame but we need to know more about the family . . . hence my interest in Lieutenant Williams.'

'Two suspects? Good for you, that's speedy work.'

'It can be the way of it, but only can be. Some cases are

solved only years later . . . if at all.'

'Well, Lieutenant Williams . . . not a popular man, not popular with his men, not popular with his brother – and sister – officers either. We now have SVPs in the navy.'

'SVPs?'

'Squeaky Voiced Persons – had women ashore for a long time, now they're at sea as well. Getting more numerous ashore lately . . . so he's not popular with his brother and sister officers. Not popular with his men either. If you're an officer, you can bully people into following you, or you can make them want to follow you by virtue of your leadership skills . . . we like the second sort, Williams is the first sort, the sort that slip through the vetting procedure. Daresay it's the same in the police force?'

'It is. Sadly.'

'Williams came to us under a cloud. He had command of a minesweeper, still in his twenties . . . destined for great things in the navy. If you're given a command of a small ship when young, you're being fast-tracked for big ship command in your forties . . . I mean aircraft carrier, that short of big ship. Then a rating assaulted him. Punched him, broke his nose, in fact.'

'Oh dear . . .' Hennessey shuddered and recalled the weight of naval discipline . . . he recalled that striking an officer was second only to selling secrets to a foreign power in terms of magnitude of offence.

'Yes. The rating got a hundred and twenty days' detention and was dismissed from the service.'

'Is that all?'

'It was a lenient sentence and thereby hangs the tale. Turned out that the rating was the ship's cook and Williams was given to bringing his girlfriend back to the ship at two a.m. or thereabouts and having said rating turned out of his bunk to cook a three-course dinner for Williams and femme. After he'd cleaned the utensils and washed up the plates he wasn't able to get back to his bunk until five a.m., and had to be up at six-thirty or seven to cook the ship's breakfast. He wasn't getting enough sleep and was working with large amounts of hot and boiling-hot food and water. Williams coming back so late and demanding the three-star treatment wasn't a one-off, it was a regular thing. Anyway, the rating snapped, made a mighty fist and Williams went sprawling. The rating opted for a full court martial, which made the affair public and the navy hates that sort of thing, really hates it. Terrible press. Anyway, in the light of the wider circumstances, the rating got his lenient sentence and Williams was "transferred shore".'

'A vote of censure.'

'Exactly. The navy has a hidden agenda, Mr Hennessey, and the sea service personnel are seen and see themselves as a cut above the shore-based personnel. There's no inherent shame in being shore-based if you're an egghead or if you have medical reasons for being unsuitable for sea service, failing eyesight is a common cause for being transferred shore to continue your service. Some personnel have been ashore all their service life and there is no shame, but to be transferred shore after an incident such as the one I described is, as you say, a vote of censure. It's an invitation to resign. And most officers would have resigned.'

'But not Williams?'

'As you see, he's still with us, and he has not achieved promotion, he's constantly passed over. This is all off the record, you understand.'

'Understood.'

'Hence me being out of uniform, just to emphasize the informality of this chat.'

'Noted.'

'I won't be making any sort of statement about this.'

'Agreed.'

'I'm doing this to cooperate. I don't like any of my crew being looked at by the police, especially an officer. I subscribe to the view that the best course of action is to offer full cooperation in such circumstances. To do otherwise only invites suspicion.'

'I could do with meeting more people like you in my professional capacity, Commander.'

'So he came to us, not HMS Halley. By "us", I mean the

concrete fleet. The navy is a close-knit community, and the permanent shore-based officers all know each other and we all felt the smack of Williams being transferred shore in the circumstances that he was transferred, and none of us wanted him as part of our crew. We have a job to do. Do you know that for every sea service man or woman there's ten people ashore? It takes ten people ashore to keep one person at sea.'

'I didn't know that.'

'It's true. The point is that shore-based service is vital, we are not a dumping ground for the bad apples. Such a practice destroys morale. Williams was transferred shore eight years ago, still with us, getting posted from one establishment to another. A year ago he came to the Halley, by then he was one of the oldest lieutenants in the navy.'

'What is he like as an officer?'

'Very repressive. A bully. He just should not have been selected, let alone identified as a fast-track-career officer. Seems to be a man who can mislead the world around him until his true nature is exposed.'

'Repressive, you say?'

'And very dismissive. In an unguarded moment he was overheard referring to the other ranks as "the cretins". He openly refers to people who make mistakes as "cretins". "Cretin" is a form of insult he employs, he's fond of the word. It seems to have some significance for him.'

'My sergeant . . .' Hennessey dabbed his lips with the napkin and placed his knife and fork centrally on his plate. 'My sergeant says that he was very upset about the leniency you showed to the young sailor who was outside the provost marshal's office when we called the other day.'

'Was he indeed . . . that's interesting.' Timmins too finished his meal. 'Enjoy it?'

'Yes . . .'

'Good, isn't it?'

'As I said, I'll remember this pub.'

'But yes, that incident says a lot about Lieutenant Williams. That lad is close to his mother, there's just the two of them.

Found out she had cancer, just diagnosed – the boy asked Williams for a few days' compassionate leave and Williams said no, on the grounds that she was not at death's door. So he went to see her for three days anyway. I can understand that.'

'So can I.'

'He came back, but he shouldn't have gone like that. There are procedures that can be used to complain, like the rating who felled Williams in the companionway of his ship . . . he had a legitimate complaint and had access to procedures that would have had his complaint listened to, and in circumstances like that, acted upon. So I fined him three days' loss of pay and then told him that the navy is his home, and like a home it works for you, and gave him seven days' compassionate and sent him back to Newcastle – he's up there now. We'll also make sure that he doesn't leave the UK during his mother's last few months. But if he did go overseas, we could get him home within twenty-four hours if necessary. But Williams wanted Able Seaman Hendry flogged round the fleet . . . that's the lad's name, Hendry. Good lad . . . he's got what it takes to go far, he doesn't need an officer like Williams.'

'Where does Williams live?'

'Here . . . in this village. You can walk to his accommodation from here. You'll meet his sister, she's up from London to help him sort out his parents' estate. So he told me.'

'What little there is to sort out.'

The two men stood outside the pub, shielding their eyes against the glare of the sun.

'Left from here,' said Timmins. 'Then first left again. Narrow lane. Yellow-fronted cottage.'

'Yellow!'

'Don't know what they call it, "burnt sand", I suppose, a dull, off-yellow, but it actually seems to fit quite well, since the fields are now yellow with oil seed. Hedgerows and the trees are still green, though, so all isn't lost.'

The two men shook hands warmly.

*   *   *

142

Hennessey left his car in the car park of the Dog and Duck and walked to Williams's rented cottage following Commander Timmins's directions. He located it easily, the only yellow-fronted cottage amid whitewashed cottages, or cottages of naked stone. He conceded Timmins was correct, the colour did work well and was not at all intrusive, possibly because it was swamped by the vast carpet of bright yellow behind it, being a field of oil seed. He walked up to the front door of the building and rapped on the metal knocker, twice, with a deliberate pause between each knock. Knock . . . knock.

The door was opened quickly, as if the person who opened it had been standing on the other side, immediately so. The person who opened the door was a tall, slender woman with short hair, who looked pale of complexion and a little wide-eyed, as if travelling a route she had never before travelled. She was clearly surprised to see Hennessey, as if she had flung the door wide in the full expectation of greeting a specific person. 'Oh . . .' she said.

'You were expecting someone else?'

'I thought it would be my brother. He said he'd try and get home early . . . or call in over lunch . . . one or the other. I'm sorry, you are?'

'Police.' Hennessey showed the woman his identity card. 'Chief Inspector Hennessey.'

'Oh!'

'You seem bothered?'

'No . . . no . . . I . . .' But her face, already pale, had drained of what little colour it had retained. 'How can I help you?'

'I'd like to talk to you, if I may.'

'About?'

'Your parents.'

'Have you caught the person who did it?'

'Getting there, one or two suspects in the frame.'

'Oh, good . . . good.'

'Can I come in?'

'Sorry . . . yes.' The woman stepped aside.

'You're Nicola Williams, I presume?' Hennessey stepped

into the cottage, finding that, just as in the Dog and Duck, he had to bow his head to avoid low beams.

'Yes. Yes, I am.'

The cottage had a cosy but cramped feel. The floor area was taken up with large cardboard packing cases sealed with scarlet masking tape. 'Moving home?' asked Hennessey.

'Well, yes . . . Please take a seat, you'll bump your head if you don't.'

Hennessey lowered himself gently into an armchair. Nicola Williams sat opposite him.

'Yes . . . the cottage is proving expensive . . . I came to be near Rufus and . . . well, just to be here . . . I have little to do until needed so I agreed to help Rufus pack his things. He's moving back onto the base . . . he doesn't want to . . .' She was nervous, thought Hennessey . . . avoiding eye contact . . . false humour . . . not really meaning that smile . . . a woman with a secret.

'Well, I won't take up too much of your time, I really called to ask you a question I asked of your brother, being, do you know of anyone who'd have reason to murder your parents? The murder, incidentally, had all the hallmarks of passion about it.'

'No.' The shake of her head which accompanied her answer was vigorous. Too vigorous for Hennessey's liking. 'What about the people under suspicion?'

'Well, they have motivation, that's for sure, but we can't link them solidly enough to charge them. We need more evidence, or we're looking in the wrong direction. We don't want to charge the wrong person, that looks bad, especially if it leads to a wrongful conviction. You'll not want that any more than we do?'

'No . . . no.' She forced a smile.

'The cottage is proving expensive, you say?'

'For Rufus, yes.'

'He could move into your parents' bungalow, it would save him some money while he's stationed at HMS Halley anyway.'

'He can't do that.' She was nervous. She seemed guilty. He

liked her for that . . . a woman with a conscience, and not an accomplished liar.

'Oh?' Hennessey paused. 'I know that a tragedy has taken place there, but once we have released it from crime scene status . . . your brother could move in there.'

'No . . .'

'But the property is now yours, I assume?'

'No . . .' Nicola Williams's hand went to her head. 'It wasn't, my parents have no money. It's going to be repossessed . . . we can take the furniture out, that's all we'll inherit, a few sticks of furniture . . . cheap stuff, at that.'

'Is that something of a surprise for you?'

'Well, yes . . . you see, I thought we had pots of money . . . they sold an enormous house, the Grange. Mummy and Daddy sold it recently and bought the bungalow. They said they couldn't cope with the large house . . . the time taken on its upkeep, not the cost, so they sold it and bought the bungalow. It didn't fit with what Rufus and I knew of Daddy, appearance means a lot to him . . . but we went along with it . . . it's their house, after all, nothing else we could do. But those poky little bedrooms . . . this entire cottage could fit into my bedroom at the Grange. It was only at the meal at the Mill last Saturday that we found out what the truth was, that our worst fears were confirmed. We both knew that Daddy wouldn't sell the Grange unless he had to, and he admitted it over the meal. He was broke. But what made it worse is that he was his usual impossible self . . . he has this ability to laugh at tragedy . . . it just didn't reach him, he was full of "easy come, easy go". It was such a drop for us . . . such a fall from grace . . . downward social mobility isn't the word, or phrase, or whatever . . . and it didn't reach him. Mummy was more down to earth . . . she looked uncomfortable . . . she said that this would be our last meal at the Mill together . . . it was, but not the way she meant it. But Daddy just ordered another bottle of very expensive wine. We had an uncle, Rufus and I, we never knew him but he drowned in the bath at his house and left Daddy a fortune . . . I mean millions of pounds . . . that was money for our future, to see Mummy and Daddy out and to secure the future for our family for generations. With careful management that was security for the Williamses, yea even unto the tenth generation, it was the foundation of a dynasty. We could have become one of *the* families of England . . . not in my lifetime, or even my children's lifetime, because these things take time . . . but my grandchildren might find that doors were beginning to open for them. We thought that that was ahead of us but all the while Daddy was . . . well, I don't know what he'd done until . . . but over the meal at the Mill we found out that we'd bellied up. We couldn't really afford the meal we were buying.'

'Hard news.'

Nicola Williams nodded. 'My brother and I, we didn't want to believe what we suspected, but when the news came it came in a single sentence. "We're broke." Mummy said it. Two words that shattered our worlds. And Daddy just smiled and said, "Easy come, easy go, let's have another bottle of the white." Daddy may not have cared but we did. We were depending on that money . . . it makes you lazy . . . Daddy gave us an allowance so neither Rufus nor myself pushed ourselves in our jobs, we didn't have to.'

'So you thought.'

Nicola Williams nodded. 'So we thought. Rufus especially, he was frightened of poverty . . . he had a phrase, "fear of drowning in poverty". He often used it. He said a man needs money like a sailor needs a ship.'

'To keep afloat?'

'Yes, that's how he meant it. A good boat under him at sea and a good bank balance under him on land. We knew Daddy had millions, we thought he was spending the interest . . . but he was frittering away the principal . . . all with his devil-may-care attitude.'

'Put a damper on the evening?'

'Did rather.'

'So you went home?'

'Yes.' She looked sheepish, avoiding eye contact.

'Straight home?'

'Yes.'

'Straight to bed?'

'Yes. It was the only thing to do. The atmosphere was tense. You could cut it with a knife. We all went to our rooms and shut ourselves off from each other, and the world. I think Rufus and I hoped we would wake up to find that it was a terrible dream.'

'When did you last see your parents?'

'On the Sunday afternoon. Rufus had left by then. I stayed on for an hour, talking to Mummy, then drove to London.'

'So you were at work on the Monday morning?'

'Yes. I worked hard. For the first time I realized that I needed my job. I also needed the normality.'

'Someone will verify that you were at work on Monday of this week?'

'Yes . . . my colleagues . . . why?'

'No reason . . . just a routine question, no need to be worried.'

'Oh . . .' But Hennessey felt her relief was palpable. 'Tell me about your father.'

'He was a queer fish. He was two people in one, hale-fellow-well-met to the world, a tyrant at home. Poor Rufus . . . when he was growing up the only thing he could do without permission was to breathe, and he was lucky to do that. Mummy went along with him, she couldn't stand up to him.'

'And he squandered all the money? Doesn't sound like a tyrant.'

'Sounds like a hale-fellow-well-met, though, doesn't it? I told you he was two personalities in one.'

'Tell me about your uncle? The one who left your father all that money.'

'Uncle Marcus?' She looked nervously at Hennessey.

'Yes.'

'He was my father's younger brother.'

'He died before his time then?'

Nicola Williams nodded. She avoided eye contact and Hennessey sensed that he was rising a deer. Suddenly, unexpectedly, he scented a chase and a shiver ran down his spine. He knew the need for caution.

'Well . . . yes . . .'

'How did he die?'

'He drowned in the bath. Dozens of people do each year.'

'The coroner returned an open verdict. Why do you think he did that?'

Nicola Williams looked uncomfortable.

A pause.

'Miss Williams, if you've got something to tell me it's really in your extreme best interest to do so.'

'It's nothing criminal.'

'What then?'

'It's an awful skeleton in the family cupboard.'

'So tell me; if it's not relevant to the enquiry it won't go beyond these four walls.'

'It's not relevant.'

'That's for me to decide.'

'He was a cretin. He suffered cretinism. He was about three feet high.'

'That's not much of a skeleton as skeletons go.'

'That's not the skeleton.'

'Oh?'

'His mother, my grandmama tried to drown him. She was what in today's politically correct times would be called a "lookist".'

'Ah . . .'

'His condition began to become apparent when he was about ten or twelve, up to then he'd been normal if a little frail . . . when cretinism was diagnosed, she tried to drown him . . . she made a determined effort, locked him and her in the bathroom . . . he managed to scream and Grandfather kicked the door in and saved his life. He grew up with a fear of drowning, hence the showers. He also had a lake filled in.'

'A lake?'

'He bought a large house which had a lake in the grounds. The first thing he did was to have the lake filled in. That's the skeleton. It didn't come out at the inquest because the family don't talk about it, let alone want it made public.'

Hennessey had a sense of having made serious headway,

but he was unsure as to the direction. 'That's a family secret?'

'Well-kept. I only found out about it last year, or the year before, when Mummy and I were walking in the garden at the Grange.'

'Does your brother know the story?'

'I don't think he does. That's where Daddy gets his obsession with appearance from, his mother was such a lookist . . . if it didn't look right it had to go. Poor Marcus couldn't live up to the Williams image, nor to the Sieff image – Sieff being Grandmama's maiden name – so he had to go.'

'Where is your grandmother now?'

'In a nursing home. Her mind has gone.'

'Lucky her, in a sense.'

'Part of me wishes they had involved the police and had her charged with attempted infanticide. Ten years in a women's prison would have done wonders for her attitude.'

Hennessey nodded. She had a sense of justice. He liked that about her as well.

That evening, Hennessey packed an overnight bag and drove from Easingwold to the village of Skelton with its tenth-century church. He parked on the road beside a rambling mock-Tudor detached house and crunched up the gravel drive. He was pleased for the owner that gravel had been laid, for his money gravel and a dog were still the best burglar deterrents by far. The garage which was built into the house, integral, he believed the word for such was, had both doors shut and padlocked. The family's car was tucked up for the night. He rang the bell at the front door and was greeted warmly.

In the house, cup of tea in hand, he sat at the long kitchen table and helped Daniel with his maths homework. It was pre-secondary school level and so Hennessey could cope with it. Just. Later he picked up a magazine for teenage girls and began to leaf through it.

'You shouldn't be reading that, George.'

'Oh?' Hennessey smiled at Dianne, fourteen, whose magazine he was reading. 'Well, you see, that's where you're

149

wrong, the quickest way to find out how someone's mind works is to read their choice of magazine – not their choice of books, or their choice of newspaper but their choice of magazine, especially the ads at the back – and I want to know what makes the mind of a teenage girl tick. I want to know what your prejudices and conceits are . . . but if it upsets you?'

'No . . .' the girl replied warmly. Then she paused and said, 'George, what happened to your wife?'

'Dianne.' Her mother turned from the kitchen work surface and glared at her.

'I don't mind.' Hennessey put the magazine down. 'She died,' he said. 'It was a long time ago now, thirty years, more in fact, she'd just given birth to our son Charles – he's a barrister now – and was already talking about number two . . . she was walking in the centre of Easingwold, that's where we lived, and where I still live . . . about this time of year . . . hot and sunny, and she just folded up . . . just collapsed . . . it was in the middle of the afternoon, folk rushed to her assistance assuming that she'd fainted. Fortunately, Charles wasn't with her at the time . . . she'd left him with a neighbour . . . but she was dead. Life had just left her.'

'What caused it?'

Hennessey upturned the palm of his hand and raised his eyebrows as if to say, 'Who knows?' Then he said, 'You see, Dianne, as I have grown older I have come to believe that if the sum of human knowledge was represented as a tennis ball, then on the same scale, the sum of what we don't know but is fact and awaiting discovery could be represented as a basketball. At the time of Jennifer's death, and still today, the best the medics could come up with was "Sudden Death Syndrome". It happens – rarely, but it happens. Often the person is a young adult in good health, they're walking down the street or sitting at home and life just leaves them. It just goes, suddenly, without warning, as if the person has been switched off. But don't fear it, there are many, many other things to fear before you need fear SDS. But that's what took my wife. She was twenty-three.'

'I'm sorry.'

'Thank you, but there's no need to be . . . I still cherish her memory and I believe that she's still in the garden she planned just before she died. I'll never give up my house because of that. Sometimes I go into the garden and sit and talk to her. I'm mad . . . but I do it.'

Later that evening, when Fiona had returned from the stables, and she and Dianne and Daniel had the upper floor to themselves and were 'shifting' themselves to bed, which involved running backwards and forwards along the landing many times, squabbling over the use of their bathroom (the house had two, one designated for adults, the other for children), Hennessey and the lady of the house sat quietly in the kitchen and Hennessey said, 'Can I pick your brains?'

'If you wish.'

'It's about work.'

'I thought it might be.'

'Cretinism. What is it?'

'Um . . .' The woman inclined her head to one side, in the manner that Hennessey had found was the way of it when learned persons speak with authority . . . the pause which speaks of knowledge. He had rapidly learned to be cautious when dealing with people who profess to have knowledge at their fingertips. 'Well, it's not to be confused with dwarfism, though in the adult it appears much the same. Whereas dwarfism is congenital, cretinism sets in at the onset of puberty, and in essence it's caused by an underactive thyroid gland. People who suffer from cretinism start out normally and then stop growing. The condition was for a long time associated with mental deficiency, but that was only because cretins were dismissed and not educated. Cretinism doesn't affect brain functioning. There's no reason why a cretin can't become an intellectual wizard.'

'Hence the use of the word as an insult or term of abuse.'

'Yes . . . it has that same punchy quality as "spastic", which is also a distinct medical condition. Spasticity, though, is still with us. Cretinism can be cured, we can stimulate the thyroid gland and enable the person to grow normally. Originally the

151

treatment was at the expense of the person's sex drive, but we've cracked that one now and normal growth in all areas is possible. Why do you ask?'

'Just a development in the Williams murder case. I spoke to Yellich, he'd been in Malton all day. He came back with some very interesting information which gelled with what I had found out during the day.'

'Really?'

'Yes . . . it's something that has crept in round the edge of the affair. It's probably not central. Found a good pub today, by the way . . . out by Knaresborough way, the Dog and Duck, excellent ploughman's, just ideal for our occasional lunchtime rendezvous.'

'Well . . .' She paused. 'It's gone quiet up there . . . shall we go up?'

Hennessey took a mug from the kitchen to fill with water in the bathroom because he found that he invariably became thirsty in the night.

'Funny,' she whispered, plucking up her long and thinly cut skirt as she climbed the stairs.

'What is?' hissed Hennessey.

'How once you were afraid of your parents, and no sooner you've stopped being afraid of them, you become frightened of your children,' Louise D'Acre explained.

9

Saturday

. . . in which Nicola Williams catches the last bus and Chief Inspector Hennessey comes across a date which has personal significance.

'It's not on, Hennessey, it's just not on. It's your neck, not mine. The Chief Constable wants a reply, so what do I tell him?'

'Excuse me, sir.' Hennessey stood in front of the man's desk. 'But I was not harassing him. Yellich went to his house and spoke to his wife.'

'That's not what Mr Richardson's solicitor has told the CC. If you're harassing anybody it weakens the case, you know that, apart from it being unlawful. What have you got on Richardson, anyway?'

'Quite a lot. Motive, possible implication with an earlier murder with a similar MO. I've made a case with less.'

'And he's in the cells now?'

'Yes, sir. As is Sheringham, who for my money is the prime suspect, but I'm not dismissing Richardson.'

Commander Sharkey reclined in his seat. A framed photograph on the wall showed Sharkey in an army officer's uniform, a second showed him in the uniform of an officer in the Royal Hong Kong Police, now he was a commander in the City of York Police. He'd done well for a man in his forties, younger than Hennessey, and Hennessey couldn't take that from him. 'Sheringham, you see, is a smug piece of work

153

but frightened of his wife, and he has motivation to murder both Mr and Mrs Williams.'

'He has?'

'They were both going to blow a whistle on him. Max Williams was involved in a drug scam, he was funding a huge purchase of anabolic steroids and seemed to be getting cold feet and may have been about to turn Queen's evidence against Sheringham. Mrs Williams was threatening to expose his marital infidelity. That's motivation enough. The other point is that they are both known to each other, they work out at Sheringham's Gym and are known to be drinking partners.'

'A conspiracy, you think?'

'I wouldn't rule it out, sir. And apart from them both having a motivation to murder Max Williams, they are both very strong, very fit men, quite capable of digging the shallow grave within the hours of darkness. In fact, they'd make short shrift of it. Very short shrift, despite the fact that the soil is baked hard and would be as solid as if it were frozen.'

'But you're still lacking the vital link in the evidential chain, are you not?'

'We've still to quiz both of them again, sir. But yes, the vital link is missing, which is why we haven't charged them.'

'Why the call on Mrs Richardson in the first place?'

'Just to take a measure of the lady, and also following up a point made by Sergeant Yellich who felt that the sanitizing of the crime scene had a woman's touch about it.'

Sharkey raised an eyebrow.

'Look, sir, we're trying to solve a murder here. No, we're not, we're trying to solve a double murder and I for one have no time for political correctness at a time like this. Especially as there is such a thing as a woman's touch, more care, more attention to detail, and, as Yellich said, Williams has ruined Mrs Richardson's livelihood too.'

'Alibi, for her?'

'None. Neither she nor her husband nor Sheringham have an alibi for the time of the murder, nor for the time of the likely disposal of the bodies.'

'All right, George, that gives me something to tell the CC.'

'Yes, sir.'

'This is a high-profile case, George. The CC wants a result.'

'Understood, sir.'

'But a safe result. A secure conviction. So please proceed with caution.'

Hennessey knew he was getting old when constables looked young, but this was ridiculous. A schoolgirl, a child . . . still slight and frail of build, still awkward, yet she was a Mrs, a married woman. She had rings on her finger which said so and she was a solicitor. Monica Have. She announced herself to the room for the purposes of the tape recording as Monica Have of the firm Have and . . .

Hold, thought Hennessey, or perhaps Have-not.

But the woman said, 'Scarborough, of York.'

Hennessey wrote Have and Scarborough, solicitors, York' on his pad.

Yellich said, 'I am Detective Sergeant Yellich, City of York Police.'

'Mr Richardson . . .' prompted Hennessey. 'For the tape.'

'Michael Richardson,' he said resentfully.

'Right, Mr Richardson, you knew Mr Max Williams?' Hennessey asked the questions, Yellich observed acutely.

'Yes.'

'In what capacity?'

'He engaged me to build a house for him.'

'For which he couldn't pay you?'

'Yes. As I said.'

'Just to get the story straight, you didn't ask for money upfront, nor for an agreed sum to be lodged with a firm of solicitors to be released upon satisfactory completion of the work, because you believed that he had the money.'

'Yes. Stupid, to be sure, but yes.'

'He had a reputation in the Vale for being a soft touch for a lot of money, is that correct?'

'Yes. He came on the scene recently, a year or two ago, but

155

his reputation got round the business community.' Richardson spoke freely but Hennessey was acutely aware that the man was not giving anything away.

'He's ruined your business?'

'Looks like it. The housing market is depressed at the moment, couldn't sell that house easily anyway, too fancy for North-country tastes at the best of times. If I sold it at all, I'd have to let it go cheap. Would recover the materials and labour costs. I've got crews to pay, the bank won't lend enough to see me through.'

'A lifetime's work down the tubes.'

'Aye . . .'

'Make anyone want to kill, wouldn't it?'

'Would it?'

Monica Have didn't give any emotion but, thought Hennessey, she was clearly, utterly focused, listening to every word.

'Well, wouldn't it? You have a motivation, a strong one.'

'Yes . . .' Richardson nodded. 'Yes, I confess . . .'

'Careful!' Monica Have glanced at him.

'I confess,' repeated Richardson. 'I confess that I felt like killing him, I confess that I am not unhappy that someone has done so, except that now I have no chance at all of recovering my debt.'

'It weakens the motivation,' Monica Have said to Hennessey. 'I would point out that my client does not have the motivation you claim he has.'

'Mrs Have.' Hennessey leaned forward. 'I would point out that your purpose is to ensure that the procedures as dictated by the Police and Criminal Evidence Act are observed. You are not here to advocate on the part of your client.'

'Accepted.' Monica Have inclined her head.

'But she's right,' Richardson smiled. 'I don't have the motive you claim.'

'Only once you've calmed down. Hot-headed, though, are you not? An Irishman with the traditional fiery Celtic blood. You were seen and heard to threaten to kill Max Williams whilst holding a two-foot-long length of scaffolding, which our forensic pathologist said could have caused the injuries.'

'Could have?' Monica Have looked at Hennessey. 'It's an important point. If you can say would have, you would be in a stronger legal position. So would or could?'

'Could,' Hennessey conceded.

'You see' – Monica Have spoke softly yet with an authority Hennessey found annoying in one so young – 'for this interview to proceed, you have to be on stronger, firmer grounds. Motivation has evaporated, you haven't got a murder weapon . . .'

'And I have to say that once again you are straying into the area of advocacy, Mrs Have.' Hennessey spoke equally softly.

Monica Have made a slow, slicing movement through the air with an open palm. 'Well, let's see how far we get.'

'We'll leave the issue of the murder weapon on one side then. And frankly, as to the motivation, it isn't really an issue if the perpetrator acts in a fit of rage, then tries to cover his misdeed.'

'I didn't kill them.'

'You know Tim Sheringham?'

'Are you asking my client or telling him?' Monica Have eyed Hennessey with a gimlet-like gaze.

Hennessey paused. 'Do you know Tim Sheringham, he of Sheringham's Gym?'

'Aye, I do.'

'Well?'

'We have a beer occasionally. Nothing more than that.'

'Sure?'

'Sure.'

'Do you use anabolic steroids to build your body?'

'No. I don't need to.'

'Tim Sheringham's in the frame for this as well.'

'This?' Monica Have said, without looking at anybody.

'The double murder of Mr and Mrs Williams.'

'Thank you, Chief Inspector.'

'Tim Sheringham's in the frame for the double murder of Mr and Mrs Williams as well as you, Mr Richardson.'

'So go and give him a hard time.'

'You both have motive, you both know each other, you're both strong men, well able to dig the grave in which the bodies were found in the time you had to dig it in, and neither of you have an alibi.'

'So?'

'And the house, the murder scene was cleaned thoroughly, painstakingly. As if by a woman.'

Richardson's eyes narrowed. 'What are you saying?'

'What I'm saying, Mr Richardson, is that with your anger towards Williams, and with Tim Sheringham's double motivation which you may or may not be fully aware of, fuelled with a little alcohol, feeding and reinforcing each other, you visited the Williamses' house, where you battered them to death, and later, the following night, you buried their bodies in a field, close to their house. Didn't you?'

'No.'

'Then you got your wife to clean up the mess.'

'No!' Richardson stood up. Yellich did the same 'You leave my wife out of this.'

'Out of what?'

'This!' Richardson sank back into his chair. 'My life is ruined, without this. I don't need to make it worse by serving life for murder. I don't want my wife's life ruined. She's done nothing to deserve this.'

'But you have. Is that what you're saying?'

'No. No, I haven't.'

'Chief Inspector.' Monica Have spoke slowly. 'I have to insist that now you either charge my client with the double murder of Mr and Mrs Williams, or you discharge him from custody pending further enquiries. You have no evidence on which to hold him, and in the absence of a confession, I have to say that your only option is that of the latter.'

Hennessey sat back in his chair, glanced at Yellich, who raised his eyebrows. He then said, 'This interview is terminated at . . . 10.45 a.m.' He switched off the tape recorder. The red recording light faded. He took one of the cassettes and placed it in the case and handed it to Monica Have.

*   *   *

Bravado.

Smug. Well turned out, muscular, handsome, smiling, holding eye contact, but inside, Hennessey knew, inside Tim Sheringham was shaking like a leaf.

The twin spools of the tape recorder spun slowly. The duty solicitor turned to Hennessey as if to say, 'A pause is a pause but this has gone on too long.' Hennessey, undeterred by whatever the duty solicitor might think, had to concede that Sheringham was bearing up well, standing up to questioning, hard questioning, very well. Very well indeed. He'd been here before, he knew the value of not saying anything he didn't have to say.

'You murdered Max Williams because he was pulling out of a drug deal he was financing, and threatening to inform on you.'

'Did I?'

'Didn't you?'

'No.'

Another pause. Beside him, Hennessey felt Yellich stiffen and then relax.

'Mr McCarty informs me otherwise.'

'Mr who?'

'Mr McCarty. Sergeant McCarty, Drug Squad.'

'Oh yes . . .' Sheringham smiled. 'I remember him now.'

'I bet you do,' Hennessey growled, fighting back a growing dislike for Sheringham. 'Have quite a motivation, have you not?'

'Have I? Not?'

The duty solicitor, a small, bespectacled man who had given his name as Fee, and who Hennessey had not met before, glanced at Hennessey but said nothing.

'You were having an affair with Mrs Williams, she threatened to inform your wife of that and she had photographs that compromised you. And he, well, he had information which could jail you and he was going to spill, he'd already been interviewed by the Drug Squad, and he was going to go along with a sting operation and you found out, or you suspected, and so you bumped them off.'

'Could you be more specific, please?' asked Fee.

'So you murdered them. Two birds with one stone.'

'Did I?'

'Didn't you?'

'No.'

'Then you cleaned the mess up, but not well enough, didn't get little specks of blood up from under the carpet.'

Sheringham remained silent. Smiling.

'Then you put them in a shallow grave.'

'Did I?'

'Didn't you?'

'No. In fact, no, I didn't.'

'But you benefited from their murder.'

'Well, yes.' Sheringham pursed his lips. 'Yes, I have. My marriage may well survive now, for one.'

'And for two, Mr McCarty of the Drug Squad won't be obtaining the major conviction he was anticipating.'

'No comment.'

'You know with that anabolic steroid stunt you seem to have skated on very thin ice and got away with it.'

Sheringham raised his eyebrows.

'But murder. Double murder is a different matter. Not so easy to wriggle out of this one, especially because we can link you with both victims. Not only that, but we can link you with a motivation to murder both victims.' Sheringham shrugged.

'Tell me about your relationship with Michael Richardson.'

'He's a mate. Not close. Met at the gym. We have a beer together once or twice a month.'

'That's all?'

'That's all.'

'You see, he had a grudge against Williams.'

'I know. He told me. But it was his fault, he should have had money lodged with a solicitor, but he thought Williams's reputation as a man with a bottomless money bag was safe enough. He won't make that mistake again.'

'Two of you together, you with a strong motivation to murder both Mr and Mrs Williams and he with a grudge. After a few pints, feeding into each other . . . then you took

160

turns to do the digging of the grave . . . two strong blokes, easy work . . .'

Sheringham shook his head whilst smiling in a classically patronizing gesture which Hennessey felt was calculated to provoke him into violence. He was forced to concede that Sheringham's ploy very nearly worked. He counted slowly and silently to ten. 'Then,' he said, 'Mrs Richardson cleaned up.'

Sheringham remained silent.

'She's a lazy woman.'

'Who?'

'Michael Richardson's wife. I've never been in her home, but Mick's forever complaining about it, fag ash everywhere. I tell you, if I did want someone to clean up after a murder, it wouldn't be Mrs Richardson.'

Hennessey glanced at Yellich, who nodded.

'You see,' Sheringham smiled. 'You can't make a case, because there is no case to make. Yes, all right, I have benefited from the murder, hers anyway, it's a neat and an unexpected solution, but that doesn't mean to say I murdered them. I didn't.'

'Chief Inspector Hennessey.' Fee spoke slowly. 'I have to move that you now either charge my client or release him from custody pending further enquiries.'

A pause.

The twin spools spun.

Reluctantly, very reluctantly, Hennessey said, 'This interview is concluded at eleven-fifty-five a.m.' He switched the machine off and the red light faded.

Hennessey left the interview room and walked down the corridor towards his office and then stopped in his tracks, as if he had received a blow to the stomach. He remained motionless. Then he recommenced walking.

He walked past his office.

He walked out of the building.

He walked the walls. Twice. But took no notice of the ancient city.

He returned to Micklegate Bar Police Station.

He went to Sergeant Yellich's office. Yellich was sitting at his desk. Hennessey stood in front of the desk and said, 'We've been looking in the wrong direction.'

'Sir?'

'We were right, there is a conspiracy.' He sat in the chair, folded into it, it seemed to Yellich. 'And you were right, there is a woman's hand in this. But it's not the Richardsons and Sheringham.'

'No, sir?'

'No. Let me get this right in my own head. Ten years ago Marcus Williams died, drowned in his bath. The coroner thought it might have been suicide, hence the open verdict. A young man was seen in the vicinity of the house at the time of his death, that same young man was a mourner at the funeral, when he wore the uniform of a naval officer.'

'Could only have been Rufus Williams.'

'That's my thinking. But Marcus Williams wouldn't allow anybody near him unless he knew them.'

'He also had a pack of very solemn dogs to protect him.'

'Hence Rufus calling on him and getting to know the dogs, getting them to recognize and trust him.'

'How did he get through the gates, boss? They'd be locked.'

'What are the walls of the grounds like?'

'About as high as this room, covered in ivy.'

'Even I, at my venerable age, could clamber over that, Yellich.'

'Yes, boss.'

'So that's how he got in. Keeps the dogs outside. Goes into the house . . . he's a big guy, strong guy, separates himself from the dogs . . . there's a dog flap in the front door, isn't there?'

'Yes, boss, easy to jam shut with something though.'

'Oh my . . . the thought of what happened next . . . picks his uncle up, carries him upstairs under his arm . . . removes his clothes without tearing them . . .'

'Like undressing a child.'

'Forces the taps on. They haven't been used for years, but

162

he has the strength to free them off. Immerses his uncle and sits on him until he drowns, but makes sure there's no bruising. Holds him, but not tightly enough to cause injury . . . then leaves him to be discovered, and he did that because he didn't know about Marcus Williams's fear of drowning.'

'That's a very solemn level of premeditation there, boss, very solemn.'

'Isn't it? But what's the motivation, why kill an uncle who has been a source of warmth, when your father has been a source of coldness?'

'Nowt so queer as folk, boss.'

'Which in this case is not the answer, Yellich. What would you kill for, Yellich?'

'Passion, boss. I don't like to admit it, but I think I could kill for passion, not so much me, but if anyone harmed Sarah or Jeremy, I could kill . . .'

'That makes you a human being, Yellich. But ponder Rufus Williams, what could motivate him to clamber the walls of Oakfield House, pat the Dobermans on the head as they bound up to him with their little tails wagging, then, leaving the dogs outside, go into the house, and to wherever his uncle is and say, "Hello, little man, I'm here to kill you." If passion wasn't the motive, what was?'

'Greed. Lust for filthy lucre.'

'Has to be, doesn't it? Either out of greed, or fear of poverty, if they are not in fact the same thing. Nicola Williams told me that her brother often used the phrase "drowning in poverty", or specifically fear of same.'

'I can see an obstacle, boss. An obstruction in sequence of logic.'

'Go on.'

'How could he know what his uncle was worth? How did he know the uncle would name his brother, the uncle's brother, Rufus's father, as main beneficiary?'

'I don't know and I don't know. At the end of the day it may be that his fear of drowning in poverty made him think the gamble was worth taking. The gamble being that his uncle was worth enough to murder for, and the gamble that his uncle either had left no will at all, or had named Max Williams, his brother, as main beneficiary in his will; either way, Max Williams would benefit. And if Max Williams benefited, so did Rufus and Nicola. Put them in direct line of inheritance and maybe an earlier access to it, which is how it turned out because both Rufus and Nicola enjoyed a stipend from daddy to supplement their salaries.'

'He just took the risk that Marcus Williams hadn't left a will naming a cats' home as the sole beneficiary. Yes, I can see that.' Yellich paused. 'But that doesn't explain what happened at the family bungalow last Saturday night. Suppose only he can tell us that. Shall we bring him in, boss? Time for a quiz session?'

Hennessey paused. 'No . . .' he said. 'No, bring his sister in. She'll be at his rented cottage doing his packing for him. She can tell us what happened at the bungalow, and not only *can*, but I've an old copper's feeling that she *will* tell us.'

Nicola Williams trembled with fear, she looked pale, wide-eyed, on the verge of tears.

Hennessey switched on the tape-recording machine, the twin spools spun, the red recording light glowed. Hennessey said, 'The date is Saturday, the thirteenth of June . . .' He paused. 'The thirteenth of June . . . the time is two p.m. The place is Micklegate Bar Police Station in the City of York. I am Chief Inspector Hennessey. I am now going to ask the other people present in the room to identify themselves.'

'Detective Sergeant Yellich.'

'Nicola Williams.'

'Miss Williams, can you confirm that you are here of your own volition?'

'I have not been arrested, if that's what you mean.'

'Do you wish a solicitor to be present?'

'No.'

Hennessey paused; he didn't know how to approach Miss Williams. He felt he could work his way round the edges in ever diminishing circles and, by that means, get to the heart of the matter, or he could cut the Gordian knot. He felt both

Yellich and Nicola Williams waiting his gambit. He decided on the latter option, risky as it was, he would cut the knot. 'Miss Williams, I have been hearing a lot about drowning lately. I have to tell you that you too are in danger of drowning.'

'I am?'

'Yes. You are in danger of drowning in criminality. I can throw you a lifeline, it's up to you to decide to catch it or not. You are standing on the side of the road, a vehicle is approaching you, it is a bus, but it is more than that, it is the last bus. You can catch it or let it go past you. The lifeline, the last bus, you have this one opportunity to help yourself. If you don't take this opportunity you start to work against yourself. If you're frightened of drowning, I suggest that you help yourself. I was talking to a barrister the other day who told me that it's always best to play with a straight bat.'

'What do you mean?'

'What I mean is that we will be reopening the investigation into your uncle's death. We now believe he was murdered by your brother. By doing so, he made your father wealthier by six million pounds, more when Oakfield House was sold. That made you and your brother stand to inherit the money in the fullness of time, in the interim you could access it to featherbed your lifestyle.'

'You've done your homework.'

'So you're catching the last bus?'

'What else can I do?' She sighed and looked at the floor. A tension left the small room.

'Not a great deal.' Hennessey spoke softly after a pause to allow Nicola Williams's reply to register. 'In fact, any other strategy will only worm you into a hole you'll never get out of. Don't drown, stay as near the surface as possible.'

'The straight bat?'

'The straight bat. What did you know of your uncle's murder?'

'Nothing for ten years, until a week ago this evening. I thought that Uncle Marcus had drowned in the bath.'

'What happened last Saturday night?'

'Rufus killed Mummy and Daddy.'

Another pause. 'I'm pleased for you, and I'm pleased for myself that you're taking this stance, but here I have to caution you . . .'

'I don't want to be cautioned . . . I'm in a state of shock . . . I still want to wake up. The only way I can come to terms with what has happened is to tell you . . . you see, it was at the meal at the Mill that we learned the truth . . . that we were broke . . . we had nothing . . . Daddy just laughed at it. He was a strange man, obsessed with petty things, everything in the home had to be "just so", but big issues, the important things in life, just didn't reach him. Anyway, we left the Mill, Rufus had gone into a cold fury . . . we drove home. I drove. Mummy was crying, Daddy was singing, Rufus was staring straight ahead, not even blinking . . .'

'Rufus could kill your uncle so as to put your uncle's fortune into the hands of your father but he couldn't control your father's spending of it.'

Nicola Williams wiped her eyes. 'If you're used to having money then poverty hides a real fear . . . it would be bad enough if Daddy had lost his money . . . but what Rufus couldn't handle was that he'd murdered for that money . . . then Daddy had squandered it. He'd murdered for nothing.'

'Poor Rufus,' growled Yellich. Hennessey glared at him.

'That money, properly invested . . .' Nicola Williams took deep breaths . . . 'What we could have had if only Uncle Marcus had drowned, if only Daddy had just an ounce of Uncle Marcus's business sense . . . if only . . .' She forced a smile. 'That's going to be the hallmark of the rest of my life . . . if only. This time last week, it didn't matter that I was a low-grade civil servant in my thirties, because Daddy's money paid the rent and bought my clothes and kept my car on the road . . . now all I've got is my salary.'

'You may not even have that.'

She shot a glance at him.

'Depending on what happened at the bungalow last Saturday night, you may be an accessory to murder. If that's the case, that's your job down the tubes; even if you escape prison, you'll be drawing Social Security.'

She drew breath sharply. 'You said you were allowing me to catch the last bus.'

'I am. That doesn't mean to say you'll escape prosecution.'

Nicola Williams clenched her jaw. 'I want immunity from prosecution in return for a complete statement implicating my brother.'

'You and your brother have the same ruthless streak, don't you?'

'Same tyrannical father, same weak mother who failed to protect, you have to become ruthless to survive. Maybe Daddy killed his brother in a sense, Rufus was just the murder weapon . . . I think I'll be chewing that one over for some time to come.'

'No deal about the immunity request.'

'Oh, I think there will be . . . I mean, I have a loyalty to my brother, but I have a loyalty to my parents, I have a loyalty to my uncle and I have a loyalty to myself. But like every other human being, I can only serve one master. Other masters have to fend for themselves.' She sat back in the chair, recovering composure, recovering confidence. 'I have not yet told you what happened at the bungalow.'

'I can guess.'

'I'm sure you can, Chief Inspector, but you can't walk into York Crown Court asking what you guess to be used as evidence, can you? Rufus won't be spilling any beans.' She held eye contact with Hennessey, then Yellich, then Hennessey again. 'You've got no hard evidence at all, have you? Nothing at all. But I can make and sign a statement that will enable you to clear up three murders. That will look good on your service record, and it'll be good for the statistics of this police force. So how about it?'

'I can't say yea or nay. The Crown Prosecution Service will have to pronounce on the issue of immunity from prosecution in return for Queen's evidence.' Hennessey spoke sourly. He knew she was right. He also knew she'd get her immunity. 'I have to give them a measure of your evidence, it's a question of letting the dog see the rabbit.'

'Turn your play thing off and I'll tell you.'

Hennessey said, 'The interview is terminated at two-thirty-four p.m.' He switched off the machine, the red light faded.

'Well . . .' Nicola Williams smiled. 'We got back to the bungalow . . . Rufus disappeared and returned with a long piece of metal, a car jack handle from the garage . . . he killed Mummy first . . . brought it straight down on her head . . . I think he did that so she'd never know the story about Uncle Marcus. It all happened quickly . . . then he turned on Daddy . . . really angry . . . told Daddy how he'd murdered Uncle Marcus . . . how he'd planned it, once he had realized how wealthy Marcus was and once he'd realized how Daddy had survived all the years by dipping into Marcus's pocket . . . he said Marcus hadn't got much of a life anyway . . . so we may as well have the money. We could use it, Marcus couldn't, with his hermit-like existence . . . what use was all that money to Marcus . . . confess I've never seen Daddy sober up so quickly . . . then Rufus really went mad, beating Daddy's brains out saying, "That was my money . . . that was my money . . . six million pounds . . . gone, gone . . ."'

'Then?'

'Then after we'd collected ourselves, he dragged the bodies into the garage and we cleaned up the mess together. He did most of the clearing up, I followed after him because he wasn't very thorough.'

'We thought . . . well, Sergeant Yellich here thought the clean house spoke of a woman's touch.'

'He was right.

'He went back to his cottage on the Sunday. I stayed behind, going over the cleaning until I felt I'd got all the blood up . . . then I went to the garage and said goodbye to my parents. So you see, I wasn't really lying to you when I told you I'd seen and spoken to both my parents on the Sunday afternoon. Then I returned to London. Rufus returned the next night, Monday/Tuesday night, put the bodies in the Volvo, drove them a little way out into the country and buried them in a field. So you see, I haven't really committed a very serious crime.'

'Accessory to murder. That's serious enough.'

'That could be argued. I didn't assist with any murder. I didn't know it was going to happen. When I cleaned up the mess I was in a state of shock, under the thrall of my brother . . . my state of mind was temporarily unbalanced . . . I would plead guilty to a lesser charge of obstructing the police with their enquiries . . . but for immunity from prosecution for that petty crime, you get the evidence you need to wrap up three murders. The CPS will go for that deal, won't they? Or is it an it? Won't it?' Nicola Williams stood. 'Now, if you'll kindly escort me back to my brother's cottage, I'll be able to collect my things and leave before Rufus returns from the base, he's drawn weekend day duty officer this weekend. You can arrest him when he returns at about five p.m. It'll be neater than arresting him at the base. And you'll know where I am . . . it's not in my interest to do anything but cooperate fully and completely. I'll let you know my new address.'

'Your new address?'

'Well, I've got some adjusting to do, haven't I? No more expensive rented flats in NW2 for me. I've got to find a damp bedsit somewhere. Maybe transfer out of London to some place where the rent is affordable for someone on my salary. Look for a rich man to rescue me. I've still got some good years in me. Shall we go?'

Yellich looked at Hennessey, who nodded, reluctantly.

Alone in the interview room, Hennessey looked at the date he had written on his notepad. June the thirteenth. Some years he anticipates the date with dread, other years it comes and goes without him noticing it, and other years, the worst happens, he realizes on the day that it is *the* date. The thirteenth of June. His brother's birthday. At least it would have been had he lived. Had he been cautious, not reckless, had the danger years not claimed him as one of theirs. It is said that the cemeteries are full of young men who don't believe it can happen to them, and Graham Hennessey, twenty-two years old when he died, was one such. A long time ago now, but each thirteenth of June it seemed to Hennessey as though it was yesterday that the policeman had knocked awkwardly on his parents' front door.